Praise for
DO NO HARM

"A psychological thriller like no other. In *Do No Harm*, with a sharp and sympathetic eye, Daniel Ochalek reveals the complex workings of the minds of his two protagonists, Michael and Gabriel. How Ochalek intertwines their stories, how he plays with the reader's expectations, the twists he unveils, is masterful, surprising, and ultimately emotionally satisfying. Like the skilled surgeon he writes about, Ochalek delicately and skillfully peels away layers of story to illuminate his characters. Ochalek takes us into the world of mental illness with compassion and care. As we get to know them, the beautifully rendered protagonists upend our expectations. This is a thought-provoking, assured debut novel. Ochalek's prose is at once lean and poetic as we come to know our protagonists and the worlds they have fashioned for themselves, both internally and externally. A thoughtful page-turner, this book is a must-read for anyone whose life has been touched by mental illness."

—Alfredo Botello, award-winning author of *180 Days*

"A harrowing, no-holds-barred exploration of modern medicine and what it does to one man's mind. May *Do No Harm* do much good."

—Liam Callanan, award-winning author of *When in Rome, Paris by the Book, The Cloud Atlas, All Saints, Listen & Other Stories*, professor of creative writing at the University of Wisconsin - Milwaukee

Do No Harm
by Daniel Ochalek

© Copyright 2024 Daniel Ochalek

ISBN 979-8-88824-524-8

All rights reserved. No part of this publication may be reproduced, stored in a retrieval system, or transmitted in any form or by any means—electronic, mechanical, photocopy, recording, or any other—except for brief quotations in printed reviews, without the prior written permission of the author.

This is a work of fiction. All the characters in this book are fictitious, and any resemblance to actual persons, living or dead, is purely coincidental. The names, incidents, dialogue, and opinions expressed are products of the author's imagination and are not to be construed as real.

Published by

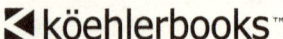

3705 Shore Drive
Virginia Beach, VA 23455
800-435-4811
www.koehlerbooks.com

DO NO HARM

A Novel

DANIEL OCHALEK

VIRGINIA BEACH
CAPE CHARLES

Table of Contents

1. Resolution 1
2. Air 4
3. I Fall in Love Too Easily 8
4. Air Raid 16
5. I'm Glad There is You 21
6. Moanin' 28
7. A Song For My Father 37
8. Out There 43
9. Blue Train 48
10. A Love Supreme, Acknowledgment 53
11. Crepuscule With Nellie 59
12. II B.S 66
13. Solitude 73
14. Imagination 77
15. The Tube 86
16. Dig Dis 90
17. The Blues and The Abstract Truth 94
18. Diamonds On My Windshield 99
19. Lush Life 104
20. Here I Am 110
21. Judgement 117
22. A Night in Tunisia 124
23. Point of Departure 133
24. Of Two Minds 136

25.	Serenade To a Cuckoo	141
26.	I'm Left Alone	144
27.	Love And Hate	149
28.	I Put a Spell on You	152
29.	Evidence	157
30.	My Ship	160
31.	Bitch's Brew	163
32.	Disambiguation	169
33.	On The Nile	174

CHAPTER 1
Resolution

"Part II Resolution" 7:17, from Coltrane's landmark release *A Love Supreme* on the Impulse label. A solo bass line introduction, then John Coltrane's saxophone slaps you in the face. It's like the listener accidentally opened the wrong door and you find yourself in the middle of it. The whole track sounds to me like an argument, two people really laying into each other. You want to get out at first, then you just settle in for the duration, to see who wins.

THIS WAS A sweaty business. I pumped the liposuction instrument rhythmically in and out, back and forth, feathering, sweeping motions. It was like the bow of a cello, except this bow was under someone's skin, in that fatty layer. Its music was a constant vibrating, and a slurping, sucking staccato. I was kneading their flesh as the tool did its work beneath my hands. By the tenth hour of each day, I could barely feel my fingers. In the evenings, sensation would begin to return. By bedtime, my fingers would be angrily throbbing, their complaints keeping me awake most of the night, only to rise at five in the morning to start again.

This is okay, I told myself. *This isn't that bad. You'll get used to it. You'll be good at it.* Such thoughts were inevitably dispelled by reality, and that truth hung in the dark corners of my mind, grinning at me from the shadows. I knew this was my last option, but even so, I never really bought into this lipo gig. I was an experienced and skilled surgeon, but I was not young anymore. I was having problems with my hands, and I hadn't been thinking clearly of late. I'd been making some poor decisions. The stress of these decisions, and the results of those choices, over the past several years, had taken their toll—physically and mentally.

The liposuction clinic was a place of business, let's be clear. It was not really a medical facility—it was a money-making machine, and I was one of its cogs. Sure, the people working there were medically trained, but for one reason or another they had found themselves on the fringes of medicine. Most of them had extensive training in what I call traditional medicine but, like me, had become disillusioned with the ever-tightening stranglehold placed upon them by government regulations, insurance company restrictions, and the dysfunctional business of medicine in this country. We had accumulated substantial debt in our medical education and surgical training. That debt is what really brought us here, this gambit. All of us doctors were only interested in the financial side of it. This was a cash business, and a very efficient one. To work and succeed as a lipo surgeon in this place was not an easy task, but it was in demand. Our society with its insecurities and vanity provided a never-ending flow of patients.

As doctors we received a modest slice of a very big pie for each liposuction patient. And we earned it. The work was physically demanding, and production expectations were high. Make no mistake, we were on a medical assembly line. There was a lot of money to be made, but to really prosper, we had to be willing to sweat and to sell our souls.

This particular California lipo clinic was tucked away on the second floor of a building, one of four modern metal and glass structures with a common courtyard in the center. There were shade trees and a garden with paths. The paths led to benches where people could take their coffee breaks or lunches. It was really quite relaxing most days. Today, however, was very much unlike most days. A news crew had arrived just behind a SWAT team. In a short time there were police vehicles and ambulances in the open space. Employees from all four buildings were running out through the tall glass doorways.

There were casualties. The shooter was at-large, no longer believed to be in the building. A sweep of the area was established as medics wheeled out the injured. The first appeared to be in extremis. They were performing chest compressions as the victim was being loaded into an ambulance. At least two others came out on stretchers—an unconscious man who, by his uniform, appeared to be a security guard, and a woman, who was awake and quite agitated and fighting the medics. Inside were casualties of a different sort—those psychologically traumatized by the events that they had witnessed.

What happened in those offices was more complicated than it initially appeared. It was the bloody culmination of decades of struggle—the triumphs and failures of a man, of family, love, friendship, of individuals, and those of entire institutions. It was life, and it was death.

CHAPTER 2
Air

"Air" 8:39, from the 1960 release *The World of Cecil Taylor*. Free dive deep, that's when you really converse with the air—when there is none. Hold your breath for the first minute-fifteen to see what I'm talking about. When you come to, it's Archie Shepp's sax shaking you. Listen. Cecil Taylor's piano sounds more like a drum, dueling with the skins of Dennis Charles. Buell Neidlinger's bass chases them till he too is out of breath.

JUST FOUR SHORT years before the events of that day, my wife and I had decided to leave everything behind and move across the country. It seemed reckless to most. Nobody really understood why we were leaving, but we did. My practice as a burn surgeon was exhausting me. I felt as though I was no longer helping people, just keeping them alive. Hospital politics was wearing me down. There were other reasons too—much more complicated ones. Back home in Milwaukee, we had the finest neighbors and friends, and we lived in a beautiful home in an historic neighborhood. In the end that didn't matter. None of these things could change the fact that I felt increasingly out of place and disconnected from everyone. We'd get together quite often, sitting on one another's porch on warm summer nights. It was perfect, actually, but still I felt alone and disengaged, staring into space while the rest talked and drank and laughed. Later I would explain to my wife how I didn't feel connected to people, not the way that other people do. I felt as though I was on the outside looking in. Inside, everyone seemed happy.

Even though I may have felt as though I know *them* very well, and enjoy them, care about them, and even love them, I felt that there wasn't one of them that could really see me. They didn't know who I was. Maybe nobody could know who I was, or worse, maybe nobody even cared to. That's what ate at me over the years. I was not like anyone else. As much as I wanted to be and tried to be, I was not.

There was another reason for my dismay, too. My wife and I no longer felt safe there. We were being harassed and threatened by someone who I thought I knew, a person that I had brought into our world, our family, someone that I loved. We dealt with it the best we could as it continued and progressed over a period of years. Our kids were young. We didn't want to uproot our lives and pull them out of their schools and away from their friends; now they were older and ready to move on to college. We were ready to move on as well.

It was to be a fresh start for us, but here in California we were never quite able to get our heads above water. At the time of our move I felt strong and capable. "California didn't know what it was in for," I remembered telling friends. Then the COVID-19 pandemic stalled my young practice.

It was during this stressful time that my wife's elderly mother died. The finger pointing and accusations among the siblings that followed started a boulder rolling that would quickly destroy the family ties that we had planned to rely upon here for the support and love and stability that we had left behind in Milwaukee when we made the move. Maybe my expectations were unrealistic, but the vacancy and isolation that settled on us after the move felt very real. Our close family here in California, meant to be our anchor, had turned their backs on us, and now we were adrift.

I was starting over professionally as well on the Gold Coast, trying to build a surgical practice from scratch as I had done decades earlier. This time, however, I was not an energetic and hungry young graduate. I was tired and frustrated and angry. Still, I felt confident in my skills and optimistic that people here would notice my abilities; I would be back on my feet soon.

Despite every effort, things didn't go as planned. Four years in, we found ourselves struggling to pay the bills, the taxes. We had done our best to make a home for ourselves here. My new practice was struggling to gain momentum. Despite feeling that I was a superior surgeon and more skilled than my peers, the truth remained that I was unknown in these new environs, and it takes years to build loyalty, referrals—a practice.

I had done it before, and it had been a battle. I was trying to do it again, to reinvent myself, but I just wasn't getting the work fast enough, and the bills were mounting. What made things worse was the loneliness. It settled like dust, when all the excitement had ended. It layered and accumulated unnoticed, day after day, until it was thick.

It took a while for that dust to settle, and with it the emptiness that replaced the family and friends from which we had run. That emptiness seemed to slowly become more powerful than even the California sunshine, and like a true anchor, it was pulling me down.

Things were tough. I guess the stress of it all was starting to get to me. A strange transition was happening so slowly that I didn't even notice it, until one day I realized that I didn't like myself any longer. I was age fifty-five and I didn't care for the person I'd become. I could no longer look at myself in the mirror. I felt as though I was becoming a cliche—a caricature. I was drinking all the time. I had a bad neck, back, and hip, and I was having nerve issues with my hands. I had spent my entire life trying to escape this very existence. In my youth I had been exposed to poverty, pain, alcoholism, and violence. It had motivated me to do something different, to do anything and everything to not end up like this. This was some cruel irony. I was starting to unravel.

Although I had twenty-five years of experience in some of the most complex and dangerous surgical procedures, I had to turn to performing liposuction as a way to make ends meet. It was a bad fit for me, and I was heading toward disaster, when fate, or the universe, karma, or maybe entropy, stepped in to stop me on that eventful day. All that I recall is that something terrible had happened at that liposuction clinic, and I am now the patient. I am now in the hospital bed, trying to recover, trying to remember.

The events are still slowly coming to me, and I know that I was seriously injured. I had been shot, and apparently, I had been close to death. After being hospitalized for months, I was only now beginning to remember things. Doctors were working with me during my physical and mental rehabilitation. They were very thorough and for reasons I am still struggling to discern, they want to know everything about me and how I ended up like this. I had time on my side, so I told them everything—every detail that I thought could be helpful, everything that I could remember.

CHAPTER 3
I Fall in Love Too Easily

"I Fall in Love Too Easily," Miles Davis Quintet Live at The Plugged Nickel in Chicago, Third Set. December 22, 1965, 11:53. It starts out soft and beautiful. Miles's weak and disheartened trumpet slurs the familiar melody. It sounds like a balloon letting out what air it has left—what it been holding on to. Then, in anguish, or perhaps in protest, it rants and complains to the bass and to the piano and the drums, who, so close to Christmas, are just trying to hold it together, and stay positive. Only Wayne Shorter's tenor sax takes its turn to commiserate.

THAT FIRST DAY of the interviews I sat waiting in a wheelchair, staring at a partially finished puzzle on the coffee table in my room. There was a bucolic scene on the box of a covered bridge in the winter. I wished that I could be in that puzzle, on that bridge. People live like that—simple, happy lives. Why couldn't I find that life? I fought off thoughts that perhaps I deserved this. Maybe it was karma finally catching up with me.

Also in the room with me was Dr. Miriam Sanders, a psychiatrist, and Detective Carlo Roman. Initially, the detective did all of the talking. He seemed likable enough but didn't smile or laugh at my little jokes. He was what my wife and I used to call, personality-free. He was a young man, recently promoted to detective. He seemed to be trying to get used to not wearing a uniform. His clothes were picked out by his wife, who seemed to be just as unaccustomed to the task. He spoke quickly, as if running late, and seemed impatient.

By contrast, Dr. Sanders had a benevolent and pleasant air about her. It was almost as though the doctor was just there to make sure that I could tolerate the interview, like she was there for my safety, to protect me. She was elegant, soft spoken and chose her words carefully and with precision. Because we were both doctors, I could have called her Miriam. But out of respect for her, and out of self-deference, I chose not to. She was my doctor, not some country club friend.

Even though I am one, I've never really liked doctors. They never seem like regular people to me. I didn't trust either one of them. But Dr. Sanders seemed to, at the very least, be empathetic. She was attractive in a nerdy sort of way, wearing eyeglasses that covered most of her face, her brown hair pulled back, wide oval eyes and lips too thin to get excited over. The detective looked like he might be Latino, his short hair wavy and dark, his skin bronze, and his chest and shoulders round and thick. He may have been a wrestler in high school. Regardless, he was serious but soft spoken.

The detective spoke first, his words abruptly shattering my daydream. "Doctor, I would like to get started now. I want to talk a little about exactly what happened at the clinic, what you remember," he said. "But first I'd like to understand a little more about how you ended up there at all. I'll be honest doc, it doesn't make a lot of sense to me, what, with your extensive training and experience. This job seems like quite a departure for you. Why did you end up working in a liposuction clinic in southern California?"

I had thought those very thoughts myself, many times. I had heard those words in my head over and over, usually screaming them in my head. Yet, hearing someone else speak those same words aloud, somehow that felt much worse.

"Well I guess you'd have to understand that I was desperate, and you'd have to understand why I was so desperate. How can I explain that to you?" I asked.

"I don't know. Try. Just tell me everything," said the detective. "Start from the beginning."

That seemed strange to me. Why so suddenly does anyone care so much about me? I furled my eyebrows at him, then glanced over to the doctor.

"I agree." said the doctor. "I think it would be very helpful for us all if we could learn about how you ended up there. Tell us everything you can remember."

So that's what I did.

FOR SEVERAL HOURS at a time over the next few days, Sanders and Roman both sat there, asking questions, and listening, as I began to try and relate to these strangers who I was, and why. It was a weird stage to find yourself upon, when you set out to relate your life to strangers—to sum it up. I'd have to say that it was a fairly unpleasant exercise. Most of those memories I would have much rather kept in the past. I started at the beginning, sort of, with my family.

"I think that families were bigger in previous decades—brothers and sisters, uncles, aunts, cousins. I was the youngest of one such clan. We were all tight and close in the early days, but by the time that I was in high school, the wheels were coming off. The happy times seemed less frequent, supplanted by arguments and money problems. Even as a young kid, I had a way of noticing things that the others couldn't, or didn't want to. To me it felt as though my family was like one of those Fourth of July fireworks, the kind that spin around on the ground, sending off a spiral of sparks until they fizzle out. My brothers and sisters and cousins, they were those sparks shooting off. Somehow, I was stuck in the center, spinning. I didn't want to be around when the fireworks ended. I sensed that it was time to plan my eventual exit. The question was how? How was I going to find a life that would follow a trajectory that would guide me out of there? I didn't want to live paycheck to paycheck, never having the things that everyone else had, never going anyplace, worrying all of the time if I was even going to have a job tomorrow.

My father was a machinist. As a kid, I had been to his factory for the annual summer barbecues, where the workers' families would come out to have a burger and walk around the filthy place, staying within the yellow painted lines so as not to get caught in any smelly greasy moving parts. I think that my father was proud of his work and of the factory. He had provided for his large family with the wages that his time and sweat had earned there. It all seemed sad to me, even as a young boy. I remember feeling uncomfortable about that. I never said a word about that to my dad, but I remember thinking, *Is this what it's about? Is this what people do? There must be something wrong with me because I can't do this.*

Yeah, I knew what he did, but oddly, I never really paid much attention to what other kids' mothers and fathers did for a living. I knew that nearly everyone was better off than my family. Their cars were not old and falling apart. The houses that they lived in were newer, with carpets, maybe a fireplace or a pool table. They went on vacations. It was clear to me that there was only one direction to go for me—up, and out.

There were only a few professions that I had ever been aware of while growing up. Engineering was one option, but I didn't even understand what engineers did. There were no television shows about engineers. My mother had an uncle who was an attorney. He was wealthy and had nice clothes, expensive cars, and two houses. He even wore a wig, according to my father. But for reasons that would make more sense to me later, I eventually convinced myself that I should be a doctor. It was a crazy idea, I guess. There were no doctors on either side of our family as far back as you'd care to look. The idea itself had come to me in such a random and silly way. I had come home after school one day to an empty house. I was the last of my siblings to be living there, so this was not unusual. I was sitting on the couch eating cold pizza and watching a television documentary about plastic surgeons who traveled to Africa to perform reconstructive surgery on children with facial deformities. It was fascinating. I couldn't stop watching it. With the confidence of a teenager, I decided right then what I was going to do. *If I can sit here eating pizza and watch this stuff without getting sick, I could make it as a plastic surgeon*, I thought.

Looking back, there was much more to it than that. Like those starving Ethiopian kids on that documentary and on the TV public service announcements, I also had been a sickly child. I spent many months in hospitals between the ages of seven to nine. I had undergone several surgeries eventually ending with the removal of one of my kidneys. Those years left me with many blurred memories; not one of them was good.

Some events, however, remained more clearly etched into my memory. The smell of the chemicals used to develop film in the X-ray department would stick with me. I can clearly recall, whenever I would have an X-ray, or later in life in my medical education and training, if I'd even pass by an area where X-rays were taken or the film developed, the chemical smell would cause me to flashback to those days when I was so ill, and all of unpleasant tests and studies that I had endured before I finally was diagnosed and eventually treated. Despite the lengthy hospitalizations and aggressive treatments, it all failed. The chronically infected kidney was finally removed to save the rest of me. You won't encounter that smell in the radiology department of hospitals today. There isn't a team of workers developing the films so that they can be thrust up on a row of light boxes for the doctors to slowly walk along and scrutinize. It's all done digitally now and viewed on computer screens. That's one thing young sick ones are spared these days—that smell.

I remembered that my parents had never told me that I was to have surgery. It was probably for the best, I guess. I was too young to understand, and would probably have been more frightened, they had thought. As a result, I was so confused by the pain that when I awoke from surgery, I had to be tied down in the recovery room like a wild animal to prevent me from disrupting my sutures or pulling out tubes or IVs. I remember those restraints, and that pain, and the anger.

Another vivid memory of the recovery room, one which was perhaps the most traumatic, was my struggling to awaken from anesthesia after one of the operations. I was in that in-between place, trying to shake off the drugs while dealing with the pain that seemed to increase as the anesthesia dissipated. Lying flat in the bed, I turned my head to the side. As my vision cleared and I was able to focus, I saw what appeared to me to be a gruesome monster in the bed next to me. I was a young boy, very much confused and afraid. I screamed and shook my head back and forth, but I couldn't awaken from this dream.

The nurses tried to calm me and restrain me. I was terrified. I thought that perhaps I was dreaming, but when I looked to my side, once again, it was still there. I immediately looked to the other side. In the bed on my left was a young boy with a calm expression. He had his head turned toward me and was saying something to me, like a whisper. I can't remember what he was saying to me, but I looked into his eyes. It calmed me, and I drifted off to sleep. Through all of these years, I've never forgotten that disfigured vision.

As an adult, I realized that the children's hospital where I had been treated was also a burn center, and that child on my right was probably a burn patient. In my subsequent career, I would become a burn surgeon. While working at an adult burn center, I would see patients like that over and over again, and every time, I would flash back to that day. I am still ashamed to recall how I had thought that the poor child next to me was a monster. I wonder if the boy survived, if he had been as lucky as me.

At the time of my illness, my mother had several other children to care for at home. She did not drive, and my father had to work. It was difficult for her to take the long bus ride to the downtown hospital. When she did come, she'd usually have a small gift for me, like a little metal car, or a pencil with a bear's head perched on top—little things. If she wasn't planning to come the next day, she'd give me change for the payphone in the hallway so that I could call her that next day. Sometimes I couldn't wait until the next day, and I would call her in the evening. I'd stand at the window next to the phone, looking down on wet pavement reflecting the streetlights and the stoplights and the taillights of the cars going by—Christmas colors. We would have whatever kind of conversation a kid has with his mom in a place like that. I think that she felt worse about her not being at the hospital than I had.

Less than two years later, in the summer, for no particular occasion, I received a gift of a pair of Disney slippers—orange Pluto slippers. Nobody in our family wore slippers. I was excited when I saw them, but then slowly, after the initial thrill, my emotion changed as I realized that this gift meant that I was going back to the hospital. I smiled, then I cried, and my mother cried, and we both knew why.

It's strange how negative experiences don't always result in dissuading the ones who experience them. Those abused sometimes become abusers. Children of alcoholics sometimes become alcoholics themselves. Young patients who spend their childhood in hospitals, in pain and frightened, sometimes they become doctors.

There may be some good that came from all of that, or at least I would like to believe so. I do know that a childhood like that can make a kid very thoughtful, and also bring a boy to search for comfort and for answers, and for the reasons why. In those years I attended a neighborhood Catholic school. My education there seemed to fit that bill. Who better to commiserate with than the handsome bearded guy who suffered on a cross for everyone. I must admit that I believed it all, and really loved it all. There was a quiet beauty and simplicity in it that appealed to me. I loved the sadness of it. Suffering was rewarded. Loyalty and kindness were weapons against evil.

I embraced all of the rituals. I was a wide-eyed altar boy. I remember during Lent, I would participate in the stations of the cross. I would walk alongside the priest, holding the massive candle, and I would listen to the words he spoke. I could visualize the tortured path of Jesus. Once, on a Good Friday between noon and three o'clock, the hours in the Bible when Jesus was on the cross, the sky turned dark and violent with storms. It left a lasting impression, one I never forgot. I had expected it to happen again every year. In subsequent Easters, during Holy Week, it didn't matter to me if the Good Friday sky was dark and windy, or beautiful blue and sunny. The fact that it had happened that one time was all that mattered. I remember thinking that religion had clear rules, and I liked that. If I followed the rules and was good from now on, I would be fine. God would take care of me."

Maybe I didn't need to tell the detective and the doctor all of this. Why do they need to know everything about me—who I pray to, what scares me? I did want them to know where I came from though, that basically I was a good kid from a large struggling family who, even at an early age, had seen enough and wanted out. My exposure to hospitals and the profession of medicine when I was a sick child gave me some direction, but it gave me some scars as well.

CHAPTER 4
Air Raid

"Air Raid" 9:17. Grachan Moncour III, from the 1963 debut album, *Evolution*. The bass is like a ticking clock, Jackie McLean's sax stirs the air. The other musicians join in and chant until Moncour's trombone speaks some truth, then it all hits the fan baby. The bombs scream as they fall to Earth. Run for your life! It's every man for himself.

FROM DETECTIVE ROMAN'S interviews with a nurse and receptionist:

They said that over the past several weeks the doctor had been acting a little strange. He would sit by himself, silently, between patient interactions, just staring off. When it was time to see a new patient or consult, or to do a procedure, it was like a hypnotist had snapped his fingers and, bang, he was on. But sometimes he seemed more on than usual, than necessary, too on.

WE TOOK A little break from the interview for lunch. I didn't go anywhere, of course. My diet during recovery was very limited due to the internal injuries and the surgeries that I had. The bullet had pierced intestines and blood vessels, eventually coming to rest in my liver, doing extensive destruction before it stopped. All of this had to be repaired. The repaired organs were slow to recover, and clear liquids were all that I was allowed to consume. None of it was very appealing—chicken broth, Jello. I stayed in my wheelchair and ate just enough of my tray to keep the nurses off my back. I could see the detective and the doctor down the hall at the nursing station. They seemed to be arguing. I couldn't hear what they were saying, and I couldn't tell you who was winning the argument, but neither of them seemed happy.

Dr. Sanders returned from the break without the detective.

"Thanks for sharing those difficult memories with us, Michael. Obviously, you made it through that period of childhood illness. I'm hoping that things were better after that," she said.

I just looked at her with a blank expression. I didn't really know how to respond. Dr. Sanders must have sensed that.

"How were your teenage years? Tell me a little bit about high school," she said.

"Gangs, racial violence, sex, alcohol and teenagers—chaos."

"That doesn't sound very pleasant." she said. "Tell me more, if you don't mind.

"I was in a fight on my first day for stepping on a senior's foot in the hall on my way to class. By the fourth year of high school, I felt as though the clock was ticking. How many more near misses before my luck would run out, before I'd get some girl pregnant, before I would get expelled, before I'd get shot?

My family had continued its descent into chaos as well. With my father's declining health and ever-increasing drinking, there was less money coming in. Private Catholic education was a luxury that was no longer an option for me. I was enrolled at a local public high school. The 1940's era brick building, sturdy and intimidating, had a student body of roughly four thousand—only a fraction of whom would ever graduate; an even smaller sliver would advance to college. The building had been transformed in recent years into something more of a detention center. There were metal detectors at the entrances and security personnel. The beautiful, oversized windows along the entire front of the building had been boarded up, ostensibly for the safety of the students.

Every day, the buses driving north would empty out the White kids, and the buses heading south would empty out the Black kids. They would walk toward the school down opposite sides of the street, not converging until absolutely necessary. Neither group wanted to be there, and they took out their dissatisfaction on each other. It was impossible to avoid violence, if only to defend oneself. The fights would escalate, as would the weapons, until somebody was really hurt badly.

In class, teachers would spend fifteen to twenty minutes of each period just trying to achieve some sort of order. That didn't leave much time for learning. Fortunately, I didn't need to learn much to put myself head and shoulders above my peers there. The bar for success was set low. These other kids didn't know it, but I was different from them. I was getting out. I would do my time there with the rest of them, but make no mistake, I was getting out. This was just something that I needed to endure.

I may have thought that I was better than the others, but I was not. I was dumb and naive, but that didn't stop me. I became arrogant and began to game the system, sucking up to teachers to win their favor. I didn't really respect them. I didn't even feel empathy for them. Like most young people, I thought that I knew more than I really did. I figured that there were only two intelligent people left in that hulking brick building—me and a quirky chemistry teacher. This man was a holdover from a different era. He was elderly, quite formal, and always wore a white lab coat. He was unfazed by misbehaving students, ushering them quickly and without emotion into the hallway so that he could resume his teaching.

He must have noticed my frustration as I tried to follow the daily lessons amidst these distractions. Toward the end of my senior year, the man took me aside after class. He told me that he felt that I had real potential, and he recommended that I apply for entrance into a private university in town. The tuition there was very expensive, and when I voiced this concern, the professor reassured me that there was a financial-aid program to which I could apply. The teacher said that he would write a recommendation for me.

I filled out the applications and was surprised when I was notified of my acceptance to the university and the financial-aid program. Weeks later, I took the bus downtown to the campus for the program's welcome assembly. It was winter and finals week for the students at the university. There was a lot of activity on the campus as students rushed through the snow to get to their exams. I remember standing tall in the aisle of the bus, holding onto the rail as the bus traveled along the street that bisected the campus. It was Wisconsin Avenue, the same street that I used to look out onto as a child from the hospital hallway window. In fact, the bus passed right by that hospital, which was only blocks away from the campus. This time I was not some sickly boy. I felt like a man for the first time that I can remember. I had an older brother who had spent several semesters there before eventually dropping out. I was going to make it through. In my mind it was a sure thing.

Once in the assembly hall, I was shocked to learn that the financial-aid program provided full tuition and money for books. Other students in the program were mostly minorities, or poor, or first- generation college students, or all of the above.

That night when my father returned from work late in the evening, I told him about what I had learned about the school and aid program. He was quiet at first. I assumed that he thought that I must be mistaken. Good fortune like that didn't happen in my family. It may have been difficult for him to see his son doing the things that he wanted to do—the things that he might have done. He was a man who had as much talent and intelligence as me, but he never went to school. He could never stay in school.

My father had fallen in love early. He was distracted by the burden of the poverty that he came up in. He couldn't focus. He drifted. He probably never realized what a beautiful choice he had made—that of love. He had everything a man could ever want really, right there. If he'd been able to see that, and remember that, he could have been a happy man. Unfortunately, he did not. Later in his life, I think that my father realized how he had lost the remarkably beautiful things that he had in his effort to grab hold of the things that he thought he had missed out on. That's a lose-lose situation.

That evening when we spoke at the kitchen table, he was a wiser man. He was in a place of knowledge, having learned the hard way what is truly important in life. I told him about the college aid package and the opportunity that I had been given. We embraced silently, neither of us quite able to believe our good fortune. I saw in his eyes pride mixed with sadness. That's a rare color—a pigment that's very costly. I will never forget those tired eyes. They seemed to say congratulations, good luck, and screw you, all at the same time. Maybe you had to be from the south side of Milwaukee to understand that sort of thing, but it was a happy moment for us both. I was starting to believe that there was a certain inertia in my life that was pulling me along. I began to believe that someone was looking out for me. I was going to college."

CHAPTER 5
I'm Glad There Is You

"I'm Glad There Is You" by Gloria Lynn. 5:25 The 1961 recording. There's an other-worldly sound to the recording, an unnatural echo that somehow accentuates the message. It's a sermon of sorts. Sparse. In a matter-of-fact way she simply lays out the facts of love. But, as she does, as she hears her own words echo in that way, she becomes powerfully frustrated, almost angry that she should even have to say these words aloud.

From Detective Roman's *interviews with OR nurse:*

The next day things started off fairly typically. The doctor interviewed the patient and marked her, then went off to mix the one-liter bags of intravenous solution while the nurses medicated and prepared the patient. The other doctors would have had some coffee or maybe they'd eat something while the patient was getting prepped, but he didn't. He'd stand at the scrub sink, scrubbing his hands quietly, over and over. He could do it for a half an hour, just staring ahead at the wall behind the sink. He would have been better served having a snack. He had gotten very thin over these past several months. He didn't look healthy.

I summarized everything, and even so, the detective seemed distracted and impatient. When he'd ask me questions, I'd look him straight in the eyes. His eyes looked like broken lightbulbs to me, each with a dark filament dangling in its pupil. He didn't care about all of the details. He wanted to know how well I had known the shooter, what was our connection, when we had met. In contrast, the doctor treating me seemed more interested than even I was. She would actually take notes, but without asking many questions. She looked at me a lot, like watching my eyes as I talked. She was one of those people who look into your eyes when you talk to them. There aren't many of those around. She urged me to keep talking. She wanted to know about college.

One requirement of the financial-aid program that I had been fortunate enough to stumble into, was that I take a summer class at the university to get a head start. There was an assumption that if we were dropped into the semester with the rest of the student body we'd flounder and sink to the bottom. Students like us needed to wade into it—hence a summer class. I was to stay on campus in the dorms, and it would all be paid for by the program.

That July I took a bus to campus with several duffle bags full of random things—the stuff that someone who has never been away from home might think essential. I checked into my dorm and threw the bags on the bed. I sat there for a while wondering what to do next. I had never lived alone. I had always had someone telling me to do this or that. I was free now, but what should I do with that, I wondered. It was exhilarating for a short while, but I quickly realized that I had nothing to do—no friends, no money. Although my southside neighborhood was only about ten miles away, it felt like a great and wide chasm between here and there.

It was summer, the campus was nearly deserted, and the dorm almost empty. I decided to walk through the campus and visit the shops along the main downtown street. I felt like an adult now, but that was more a feeling than a reality. A girl that I had dated in high school had given me a life-size poster of James Dean. I hung that on my dorm room wall, but the place still looked empty. It needed some more character. Maybe I would have a girl up there sometime, or maybe my neighborhood gang would want to hang out here. I wanted to buy something of my own now to personalize my room. I browsed through the merchandise at the shops, and browsing was about all I could afford. So I settled on a stylized brass turtle, smaller than the palm of my hand. Its shell opened on a hinge to provide a tiny storage for little somethings. I was a little embarrassed and even depressed by this shopping trip. On my walk back to the dorm I had much less enthusiasm than the positive energy I had taken with me to the shops. When I got to my room, I placed the turtle on the desk. It was so tiny and insignificant. Isn't it strange that I still remember that day and all of those silly details? It's funny, but in the years to come I would store buttons in that turtle, then collar tabs. I still have it, and I have always displayed this silly sentimental trinket in a subtle way, somewhere in my apartment or home to remind me of those days, and of how far I had come.

It was late afternoon when I returned to my dorm. On the way back I had stopped at a Walgreens and purchased a pair of haircutting scissors. I stood in front of the full-length mirror in my room and cut my hair as short as I could, the messy curly lengths falling on my shoulders and bare feet. I wanted a new start, and I thought that this symbolic gesture would help me get that. I did a terrible job however, and I immediately regretted my actions.

As the summer day gave way to dusk, I stood there with my new accident of a hairstyle and looked down from my fourth-floor window. Below, I saw people going to the movies, to dinner, to a party. They were all in couples or groups. None of them was alone. I put on an old

Gloria Lynne record and lay in bed. The setting sun turned the ceiling and walls of my room orange. The old recording had a vintage echo, and the sad lyrics mixed with the traffic and the distant conversations and laughter from the street below, creating cruel juxtaposition. At that moment, being an adult did not seem like such a great thing after all, at least not for me.

That same orange sun rose the next morning. It had been a long and lonely night, but in the warm glow of the morning I began to feel lighter. By the time my first week alone in a dorm passed, I felt a renewed sense of purpose. On Saturday, the following weekend, I took the long bus ride back home to see my mother. I brought a sack of dirty laundry. I would do my wash, hang out with my mom, and before I left for the bus stop, I would pick up some more jazz albums from my father's collection. He never listened to them anymore, so he wouldn't miss them. Although without intention, those records had imprinted jazz onto my soul, providing me a lens, however flawed or scratched, through which to view the world and experience emotion.

As I was leaving the dorm that morning, in the hallway of the fourth floor I encountered a fellow student from the program. He was staying down the hall and was exiting his room. He was quiet with an angry look. He had a bicycle hoisted onto his shoulder and strode with determination, as if heading out to right some kind of wrong. He looked how I felt, and I liked that. He barely nodded to me as he passed by. I would later learn that he had immigrated with his family from Peru as a young boy. His history was complicated and difficult. His name was Gabriel. We would eventually become close friends, the best of friends actually, and he would be the only friend that I would make in my four years at the university.

WHEN THE SUMMER ended and the fall semester began, I felt like a different person. The weight and dread that comes with transition seemed to have been lifted, and it had been replaced with enthusiasm and potential. In fact, college seemed to be everything that I had hoped it would be, at least initially. It was also many things that I could never have foreseen. Despite free tuition and books, I still could not afford to live on campus. I had to return to my childhood home. I had fallen back down to Earth. The home was now vacant of joy. It seemed as though the happiness had packed up and moved on without me, just as all of my older siblings had. It was just me now, and my parents. This was an early introduction to the harsh nature of change—the excitement and uncomfortableness of it. I was changing for the better while the world that I had loved was disappearing. Things would never be the same again. The love in that house turned quiet and weak, but I could feel it still. I was never ungrateful to my parents for providing me a home. They always did the best that they could for us, and even as a boy I had been grateful.

I commuted by bus to campus every day. The public high school education that I had endured had done very little to prepare me for the challenge of college. I had learned plenty about gangs, weapons, girls, drugs, and even some chemistry, but I had no knowledge of literature, or world events, history, or geography. My excellent high school grade point average and the honors program had been a sham. Yes, it provided me entrance into this institution of higher education, but it did not prepare me for the rigors of college-level work. I began to feel as though I was an impostor—a fake. I did not belong there, and I feared that eventually I would be found out.

I was desperate to catch up to my new cohort. I would watch the network news every evening, slowly finding out what was going on in the world, and where. I read my literature assignments, and my history text. I devoured philosophy and theology, believing that each principle or theory that I had just read contained the answers to life—until I'd read the next. I was actually learning. For the first time in my life I was being challenged, and I couldn't fake it, or fool anyone. If I was not an impostor, I would have to prove that now.

As my hair grew out, I began to look less strange, some may even have considered me attractive. Still, I had an edge about me, and I was quiet and suspicious of the new class of people with whom I found myself. I tried to fit in, thinking that maybe I could fool everyone, including myself. I brought my neighborhood high school buddies to a fraternity party in an attempt to make the most out of this new environment, maybe meet some people, find a girl. That had always worked for me in high school; get drunk, maybe get into a fight, impress some girl who wanted to date a bad guy or to piss off her father. Me and my hoodlum buddies looked the part, like a bunch of street punks among these wealthy young college students. This time however, we weren't impressing anybody with our fake toughness, raggedy clothes, and weird hairstyles. Nobody cared. We were invisible to these college kids who had come from an entirely different world. They didn't go to shitty public schools. They didn't live off campus with their faltering parents. They didn't take a public bus to campus every morning, and they certainly were not impressed by guys like me. They didn't even see me.

I couldn't think of anything worse than being invisible. I realized immediately that I didn't fit in there, in that scene, at that school, in that world. But what choice does a person have? We didn't ask to be here, yet here we are. I told myself that it didn't matter. I would show them all in the end, I decided. I was going to be a doctor. I was going to force my way into their world, eventually. Until then, I would stick with the people that I was most comfortable around—the poor, and the first-generation college kids like me, and the minority students, all of us in a foreign vessel funded by the government to bring us to the shores of success, no matter what.

That may have been the last time that I hung out with those guys. While I was off at college, my old neighborhood friends were selling cars, working in warehouses, playing music, taking drugs, and getting married. There was not enough space in my head for them anymore, really. It was filled with equations and theories, essays, and assignments. I was no longer distracted by anything. I was focused. I put the chip squarely upon my shoulder and cast off. I was afloat and drifting away.

CHAPTER 6
Moanin'

Art Blakey and The Jazz Messengers. "Moanin," the 1959 recording 9:30. Let's get goin' like a walk down the streets through the neighborhood, head up high. Lee Morgan's trumpet, sharp as snapping twigs, starts some good-natured trash talk to the people as we pass. Benny Golson, you can imagine him sitting on a stoop, calls back "Hey, what you say?" Bobby Timmons' piano saves a brawl and puts them both in their place. The grumpy bass of Jymie Meritt puts out a hand to shake.

From Detective Roman's interview with OR nurse:

The day started fairly routinely. He made jokes and sang along with the music. This particular patient was more uncomfortable than most. I had to keep holding her hand to calm her. He leaned over and said something to her, in her ear. Then he waited a while before starting again. She seemed calmer then. I didn't know what he said to her. He could be very calming to the patients. It seemed strange that something he said to her could get rid of the patient's pain. I began watching his movements. He wasn't doing anything differently, but he had just stopped talking to us and to the patient, stopped singing—just working, sucking.

Detective Roman couldn't relate to me. It was obvious. Maybe the doctor couldn't either. But I wanted them to know what I was about. They needed to know that nothing ever came easy for me—not ever. For as long as I can remember, I had to work as hard as I could for anything, and still it wasn't happening. Even now, after all of these years practicing medicine, after all of the surgeries that I'd performed, I had to keep reinventing myself. I had to be tough, and smart. I had to always find a way, always.

I kept going with the story. I told them more about college, and about Gabriel.

As time passed, I had settled into a routine. I couldn't keep up with the lectures and still be able to take notes at the same time. I wanted to just sit there and listen and watch, like you do in a movie, but I had to have notes as well to prepare for exams. I bought a handheld tape recorder. I would record the lectures and later that evening I would transcribe the recordings into organized notes. This way, I could sit there and stare at the professor, and take it all in. That's how I learned. When they spoke, I would see pictures in my head. I could remember those pictures, but they wanted words on the exams. I knew that later I could listen to the tapes and make notes. It was like going to every class twice, but I didn't care; whatever it took to get that *A*.

Evenings were spent in the various libraries about campus, smoking, drinking coffee, and studying. It's amazing how little you need to eat when you have caffeine and nicotine. Fortunate, because I had very little money for anything else. My favorite spot to study was the library in the dental school. It was ancient, and it had these little metal study desks. They were literally placed among the bookshelves, a hidden alcove. It was as though you were part of the building itself when you were studying there. I liked it there, especially during the day when the sun cast shadows down the long aisles and warmed me there, among the books. I doubted many other students appreciated it like I did as I was usually quite alone there.

Another of my favorites was the law school library. It was the complete opposite of the dental school library. There was a huge open space in which to study, with long wooden tables that stretched at least twenty feet. The tables had ash trays on them so I could smoke as much as I wanted to. There were high ceilings and long windows that looked out onto Wisconsin Avenue. Huge, ancient oil paintings hung on the walls, long and dark paintings that I could stare at for hours.

Often on Friday evenings, I'd be studying in that library, a perfect place to find the loners. What better way to pass time, convincing yourself that you are doing something more important than everybody else? The rest of the students would be going out to drink in campus bars or heading to parties. I'd be in the law school library with a few scattered oddballs, smoking cigarettes at one of those long wooden tables, gazing at one of those dark oil paintings of some nameless figure. Sometimes I would end up as unintentional bait for one religious group or another. They would send out their soldiers to recruit another vulnerable loner from the Friday evening library outcasts. It even worked on me a couple of times, but I'd only last for a few meetings, which would typically consist of us all sitting around on mattresses in some almost vacant apartment talking about the Bible. Eventually, things would get weird, and I would stop going. They would find me in the library again and try to get me to resume attending. Then there would be threats, typically regarding eternal damnation or some form of righteous retribution from God. Eventually, they would give up and leave me alone.

I think that I missed those days when I was younger—a true believer, praying to the blue-eyed Jesus, drinking the wine in the sacristy, ringing bells and lighting incense. I missed those days. I guess that a small part of me thought that maybe I would find some answers in one of those groups, but I think more likely I was just looking for some human contact.

As I said, I didn't have much money in those days, mostly because I didn't work much. It was my choice. I spent most of my time studying. I worked a few hours every weekend bartending, just enough to buy coffee and cigarettes. This routine and chemical combination seemed to work for me. My grades were very good, especially in the pre-med science classes, such as biology, chemistry, and physics.

In the summers I would work real jobs. After my freshman year, like my brothers before me, I took a job at one of the factories where my father worked as a machinist. He typically worked twelve-hour days, five days a week. He was employed at two factories. He'd work eight hours then drive to the other factory and work four more hours, arriving back home around eleven o'clock at night. I guess that's how a guy without a high school diploma raised a huge family back in those days. He knew that was the deal, and he accepted it.

My father accomplished his goal. His children were never hungry. We didn't have anything extra, or anything fancy, but we had the necessities, and we were happy. We should have been more grateful though, but it took some years for his kids to appreciate what he had done for us day after day. Yes, my father had made his bed in life, but that didn't make it any easier to lie in it. Unfortunately, the drudgery of survival destroyed him, and his marriage. Ironically, even having witnessed this, all of his children, including me, in some way seemed to copy my father's fatalistic mentality, pretty much to the same end.

When the summer came along, my father would put in a request to his boss, Shelley, like the English poet, but he was no poet. He was a hard-ass, blue-collar guy. He and my father both had forearms like Popeye. Shelley would then do my dad—his old faithful workhorse—a favor by hiring his son for a summer job, sweeping floors, and building crates for the large bearings and other automotive parts made there. I worked at my father's second factory job, but I worked the first shift there, finishing when he was just starting. Usually I would be gone before he arrived, but sometimes not. I preferred not to be there—not to see him. I guess I didn't want to see him limping toward me, down the painted aisles of the factory floor, with that tired smile. It made me feel terrible. What do you say to your dad? "Hi Dad. Thanks for busting your ass all of these years. See you at home tonight." Right.

The guys at the factory called me college boy. It was said with part humor, part resentment. Despite my free ride at the university, my father had told coworkers that he was putting me through college—paying the tuition on his factory wages. I know this because that was something that they said when they taunted me. It bothered me initially, but eventually I didn't mind. He had sacrificed plenty for me. Why shouldn't he have some scrap of dignity for all of his other sacrifices? So, I let the jealous factory mob jeer at me as if I was a spoiled college kid. Their resentment felt similar to how I viewed the spoiled, privileged kids attending college with me. I never set the factory workers straight about that, and I never said a word about it to my father.

The next summer I decided that I could not do that sweaty factory gig again—not with all the emotions and angst. I did appreciate at the time, perhaps subconsciously, what that job represented. It was a cinderblock prison filled with frustrated people who didn't have any say in what was going to happen to them tomorrow or the next day. To me they seemed like passengers on a ship that was sinking so slowly that they didn't even realize it. My dad was right there with the rest, but he knew that doom was on the horizon, and that surely made his factory imprisonment feel worse. I knew better than all of them, including my father, and I was jumping ship. From that point on, I would do anything else, even working construction and tending bar.

THERE WAS ONE job that was different than the rest. The summer before my final year at the university I secured a sort of apprenticeship at a local brewery in the microbiology department. This job involved the use of brewery yeast in the production of proteins to be used in the food industry. The genetic code for this particular food preserving protein had been inserted into the yeast's DNA. It was my first white-collar job—a job that I had secured with my brain and my education. More importantly, it exposed me to an environment where science is intertwined with industry, a collaboration where one could earn a living with his brain.

The job paid better than any I had ever had, and the brewery provided each employee with a free case of beer every week. I impressed people there early on with one of my ideas regarding the maximization of the fermentation to get the yeast to produce more of a desired protein. It was mostly a lucky guess on my part, but they thought that I was quite a young prodigy. I really had no other good ideas after that, but that one idea allowed me to coast until the next semester began.

After that first summer, when the school year resumed, I continued to get very good grades in my honors courses and in my pre-med curriculum. As it turned out, my friend Gabriel, the oddball like me who I met that first summer on campus, was also pre-med, and we were often in the same classes. That's how we began to get to know each other and eventually became friends.

GABRIEL HAD COME from Peru as a young boy with his parents and two younger sisters. Through a combination of government social services he had been able to attend private Catholic schools. But, from what I learned from the stories that he later related to me, he had always been the poor kid in class—the kid who wore plastic bags in his boots in winter, the one whose clothes were secondhand and threadbare. He had been ridiculed or patronized when playing football or basketball. It seemed as though he'd grown up friendless. No wonder that he too had a chip on his shoulder—maybe the whole brick.

His mother was a sweet and quiet woman with a thick accent and a strong will. She had the determination to achieve happiness for her children. She worked as a teacher's assistant at the Catholic school that Gabriel and his younger sisters had attended. She prized education and instilled the same values in her children.

Gabriel's father, whom I had never met, was apparently quite the opposite. He had been a detective in Peru but could only find unskilled labor work here. At some point, he began beating Gabriel's mother and abusing his sisters. When Gabriel, with his angry face, was finally old enough and strong enough to stand up to his father, he tried to right that wrong. It didn't go so well. Gabriel was beaten, and humiliated. But, perhaps the next time, or the next, he would succeed. Maybe his father realized this. Whatever the reasons, his father soon left the family, and headed to Miami where he became involved in the illegal drug scene. Gabriel told me that his father had been a corrupt detective in Peru, so crime was a very natural career choice for him. They would not see him again.

At the university, Gabriel struggled with his grades. Eventually, we studied together using my technique of recording and transcribing the lectures. Soon his performance on the exams improved. We both wanted to be doctors, and we both loved jazz. We'd listen to tracks and describe to each other a scene that we felt the music produced in our heads, or we'd guess what the performers were trying to communicate. Then we'd usually burst out laughing at each other. Sometimes the description would be so spot on, maybe too close to a truth, and there would only be a silence that said *definitely man*. We both felt like outsiders, which strengthened our bond. We became very close.

Sometimes, I'd be invited to dinners at Gabriel's family's apartment. It was small and shabby and in a rough neighborhood, but to me it seemed to be a happy place. He had befriended a local priest who hung out with the neighborhood kids, lifted weights with them, and saved their souls. Gabriel introduced me to everyone who was important to him. I was accepted by his family and by the neighborhood as someone to be trusted, someone loyal.

Unfortunately, despite our team approach to studying, Gabriel still struggled with the pace of the courses. Sometimes I just couldn't find a way to get him to grasp a concept. He would describe to me how, at times when he was thinking too hard, he'd feel his brain become numb, or work slowly like thick gel.

"Do you know what I mean?" he would ask, repeatedly when trying to grasp something beyond his ability. As our courses became more difficult, Gabriel fell behind, dropping classes with which he had struggled. By the time that I was graduating, it was apparent that Gabriel would need another year to finish.

Commencement came, and I moved on, leaving Gabriel to struggle through his final year on his own. I didn't know much about how he faired that last year as I was busy moving on to the next phase in my education. I'd reach out to him and check up on him, and we would occasionally go out for a drink to catch up. He told me that he had met a girl, but she had split up with him after a short while. His sisters were all getting older and didn't seem to need him as much anymore. His mother was dating another teacher at her school. He confided that all of this made him very lonely and that he struggled on his own. I began to feel that I had abandoned him and had wished that we could have kept moving forward together.

He told me that he was having trouble sleeping, but he had found something that helped. In the evening, lying in bed, he would read poetry. His favorite was a collection of poems by Charles Bukowski. He'd usually read a single poem right before going to sleep. The reality portrayed in Bukowski's poetry was sometimes harsh, but it was just as often beautiful and vulnerable. The poems usually made him cry, but sometimes laugh. I didn't like hearing that. He told me that the sad beauty and genius of those poems somehow calmed him. He told me that as the unread portion of the book became slim, he began to experience a sort of panic. What would he do when he's run out of pages? He would never find anything as beautiful to read again. *How will I fall asleep at night?* he'd ask himself. He finally decided that he wouldn't try to find something else that was as good as those poems, but instead, he would just keep reading the book over and over, and that finally calmed him.

As a bookmark, he used an old postcard from a north wood's supper club. These were old fashioned restaurants popular in rural lake towns of northern Wisconsin in the 1950's and 1960's. They served thick steaks and stiff drinks. He couldn't remember where he had found the card. It was old and faded, with the unnatural colors typical of photographs from that era. On the postcard, couples sat at tables covered with loud multi-colored floral vinyl tablecloths. The ceiling was low. An antler chandelier hung in the center of the room. The walls were paneled in wood veneer. The people were happy, their smiling carefree faces a strange contrast to the poems in that book. When the words got too dark or heavy, he would pause and look at the postcard. He'd try to transport himself there. Maybe that's really what helped him to sleep.

CHAPTER 7
Song For My Father

"Song For My Father," Horace Silver, October 26, 1964. You might just as well call him *Daddyo because* that's what's coming down. This entire tune is laying out the facts man, with his rhythm section: Teddy Smith and Roger Humphries. Horace plays the facts like he's sitting at the kitchen table, and just when you think he's done, it's like your mom stood up from behind him as Joe Henderson on tenor drives the message home. By the last twenty seconds it's like Horace is pounding his fists on the piano.

FROM DETECTIVE ROMAN'S *interview with several nurses:*

The case ended and he disappeared. He was soaking wet with sweat, so we assumed that he went to change or something. But he never reappeared. Nobody could find him for quite a while. We had several more patients that day. They were all lined up for him. I walked into the prep room where he mixed up the anesthetic bags. He was sitting on the floor with his back to me laughing quietly to himself. He was laughing. Maybe he was crying. It seemed like he was murmuring something. I asked him if he was okay to go ahead with the next patient. He paused then said, "Just keep em rollin'."

Detective Roman was back, his game face on, looking serious and concerned.

"I think it's time you tell us a little more about your friend Gabriel," he said.

"I have already told you about Gabriel and his family. Why are you so interested in Gabriel? He was my friend." I became agitated. "Shouldn't you be out there looking for the person who shot me—the guy who did this to me?"

"The detective relented. "Alright, we can talk more about Gabriel later. For now, it would really be helpful if you could try to remember more about exactly what happened the day of the shooting."

I had repeatedly tried very hard to remember the events of that day. The more that I tried, the worse my head felt. Each time Dr. Sanders would instruct the detective to back off or change the subject to keep me from becoming agitated. My brain was fuzzy; maybe it was the meds they were giving me. It felt like I was trying to learn how to play the piano again.

When I was a teenager, I took piano and saxophone lessons. If you're not a musician you might not know this, but when you play piano you have to read two lines of music at once—one for the left hand and one for the right, then you have to play those two different lines with the two different hands—at the same time. For the right kind of mind, maybe introduced to this at a young age, the technique isn't so weird, but for this teenager it seemed impossible. I couldn't learn how to play the sounds that were streaming in my head, and I couldn't afford enough lessons to bring piano playing within reach. I gave up the keyboard but stuck with the horn, which felt more natural. And the sax was the weapon of choice for some of the jazz stars and bands

I had come to idolize.

My frustration with the piano is how Gabriel must have felt when struggling with some of our college courses, as if there was background static or vibration in his brain, preventing him from thinking properly or absorbing the information. Fortunately, for me college was not like playing the piano. I had truly loved my studies. I thrived on the knowledge to be had there. I felt as though I could learn almost anything if I could just read about it. I would go to the campus bookstore to buy the required materials for my classes and find myself buying books for classes that I wasn't even attending because they interested me.

Literature, philosophy, theology, creative writing, even history called to me. What's funny is, not once did I have to talk myself out of buying a chemistry book or find myself astray in the section on physics or genetics. Those subjects came easy to me, but I can't say that I was ever passionate about them.

Since I couldn't remember anything about Gabriel useful to the detective, the doctor asked that I tell her about how I made the decision to carry on with medical school.

I HAD BRIEFLY entertained the idea of abandoning my pursuit of becoming a doctor for a career as a jazz musician, or, perhaps, a major in philosophy or maybe history. One night, when my father came home from his second factory job, I met him in the kitchen, and we discussed how my classes were coming along. I told him that I was thinking of maybe being a history professor. I saw a combination of pain and anger in his eyes. There was a difficult silence, followed by a sort of eruption.

My father sternly reminded me that there was no money to be made teaching and probably not in blowing the sax—even as much as he loved jazz. No, I was to be a doctor, or I'd spend the rest of my life working physical labor like him, struggling to pay my bills as my body slowly gave up on me. I knew that choosing a life of labor would lead to increasing bitterness—in my father's case alcoholism, which had afflicted every other man in my family. Eventually I would die penniless, miserable, and alone. That isn't exactly what he said, but that was the message. There was much pounding of his large, calloused fists on the kitchen table to bring the message home.

He was right. Although the argument seemed exaggerated for effect, it was quite persuasive. Of course, there were other options. We never discussed the countless examples of success that were to be found all around us—the business owners who started out as plumbers or electricians or carpenters, or the mechanics who owned their own shops. Perhaps a trade would have been a better fit for me—problem focused, dealing with real people. Maybe I'd have been happier not trying to force myself into a world where I didn't belong and couldn't relate to. But it wasn't that simple. I never really fit in with any crowd.

My father was the same—a guy who read poetry during his break time at the factory and made wine in our musty basement, and who listened to jazz for countless hours. We were like gypsies. People like us never fit in with any group. There were aspects of his life that would make the people around him scratch their heads, and I was very similar. I resisted his coercion, but the daily examples that my father provided, those of fatigue and frustration, proved quite convincing. He had put so much pride into the very idea that his son was to be a doctor that it was as if he himself would be attending medical school. He couldn't bear to see it not come to fruition, and I couldn't bear to disappoint him.

When the time came to apply for admission to medical school, I cast my net as far as I could, desperate to start anew in some exciting and unknown location. Someone up there had always watched out for me, so why not apply to the best—the Ivy League universities, maybe Stanford or a top school on the West Coast? I had graduated with honors after all. I was optimistic. I was confident.

When it was all said and done, I interviewed at some programs far from home, but none in the Ivy League. I was offered a spot at one of the California universities, among others. The out-of-state schools were expensive, and this time the government would not be picking up the tab. Being a first-generation college graduate seemed to be inconsequential for med school admissions. I had to be practical. The biggest and best schools came with the highest cost of attendance—even if I did get in.

Eventually, I put on one of my father's vintage wool sport coats and interviewed for admission to the local medical college in my hometown. After I returned home from the interview, I stood at the kitchen sink looking out of the small window into the backyard that I'd grown up playing in. It was now neglected and overgrown. It was a bittersweet moment. I felt as though I was settling. I was afraid to take the risks required to break out, go into debt, escape. I remember telling my mother that the interview had gone really well. "They loved me, Mom." I had decided to accept their offer, and my mother was very happy to hear that. She assured me that I could continue living at home to minimize the amount of loans I would need. That was always the mindset in the machinist's household. It was a survival mentality. Having lived our entire lives in that way, it was difficult for any of us to think any other way. Although I was again grateful for this offer, I knew that I would need to move out. If I was not going away to school somewhere exciting and new, at least I would get out of that house.

I planned to move into an apartment with my girlfriend. Yes, I had met a girl. We were quite similar in our personalities and interests. It's not that she was interested in medicine or in being a doctor, but we shared creative interests and had similar temperaments. She was from an equally inhospitable area on the other side of town. To make something of yourself coming up in those neighborhoods you had to do it yourself. We shared that mentality, and now we had each other. This alliance—having someone to split life's burdens—put us one step ahead of most of the kids we had grown up with.

I had seen my siblings all leave my parent's house one by one. Some departures had been smooth, others not so; that would be how my move would go. Once my father learned about my plans to leave, he actually stopped speaking to me. One day, quite unceremoniously, I loaded my car with a few boxes, kissed my mother goodbye, and left. I was only moving downtown, but I might just as well have been leaving the country. It was some time before he and I spoke after that. It was never discussed, and at the time I didn't really understand my father's behavior. Whatever the reasons, our relationship was never quite the same after that.

Years later, when my own children would leave home, I would begin to understand my father more clearly. I would understand the feelings of this man who had put so much of himself into creating a beautiful and strong family that stuck together and loved each other and fought for each other, only to see it deteriorate into ruins. His adult children were now making their own way and fighting their own battles with little interest in each other. The home that had once been filled with those people and that loyalty was now all but empty. At the end of the day, he had seen it all taken away. One after another we left him. This last one hurt the most, if only for being the last. He hung that on me. He couldn't help himself. I didn't deserve that responsibility or the guilt for moving on. At the time I didn't fully understand his perspective and vitriol. As I told my story to the doctor and detective, I realized that now I do.

CHAPTER 8
Out There

Eric Dolphy's 1960 release "Out There" 6:52. The alto sax sounds like a fly or mosquito, at times a bumble bee. When you don't know where you are anymore, you're out there.

FROM DETECTIVE ROMAN'S *interview notes with various clinic staff:*
The next day he seemed back to normal—joking and smiling. The nurses saw him eat something. That's kind of the way it went for quite some time. There were days when everything was good, and there were days when things were not good. The nurses and other staff said they could never see them coming, those bad days. Sometimes it would all change in an instant.

THE DETECTIVE SAT quietly the next morning, barely making eye contact with me, until he suddenly slapped his notebook closed and looked up. "Let's pick up where you left off. Tell me about medical school." Without reluctance, I started. If nothing else, sharing my story, however, successful, or miserable, was cathartic.

Medical school education became another episode of a repeating theme. Again, I found myself in over my head. This time, the volume of coursework and memorization was so demanding that there was no way that I could record and transcribe all of the lectures; nobody could. That's the way medical school had always been—impossible. To make it possible, a system had long ago been developed to help students learn, or at least memorize as much as possible.

The entire medical school student body participated in a note-taking service that was coordinated by a small number of students. Each student in the larger group was responsible, on a rotating basis, for recording and transcribing an outline of a given lecture, usually once or twice per month. The transcripts would then be circulated by those in the smaller group to all of the students. Even with this study service, I felt overwhelmed by the amount of material we were expected to digest. The pace was grueling, and I was certain us students were not actually expected to retain all that was being crammed into our heads. It seemed impossible. I was sure of this right up to the point that I almost failed all of my first exams. Three or four exams were taken on a single day—gross anatomy, embryology, histology, physiology. Apparently we were, in fact, expected to learn and retain it all, and I was going to have to find out how.

Again, I found a way to change my routine—more cigarettes, more coffee, less sleep. Minus the cigarettes, this is what we all did. The constant struggles had made me insecure. I began to constantly question my abilities. I was not alone in this. We were all struggling but some of us were just better at it. Some of us took comfort in a joke: "What do you call the person who graduates last in his medical school class... doctor." We stuck together and helped each other out, but I could not escape the feeling that I was the one that didn't belong here, that I was a fake, and eventually everyone would realize that.

At the end of that first year of medical school most of the students spent the summer working on medical research or in some sort of lab—something that would bolster their resume. Not me; I drove a truck. I was mentally exhausted, and I really needed the money, so I spent that summer driving, delivering, stocking, smoking, and losing more weight. I recall one summer day, between deliveries, I pulled my truck up to the medical school front doors so that I could run in and take care of some forms that needed my signature. Many of my fellow medical students were sitting outside having their lunches. I flicked my cigarette butt out of the open window, put the hazards on, cinched up my uniform pants, and shuffled by them. I couldn't help but laugh at the looks on their faces. In the end, driving that truck served me much better than any research project or externship could have; it reminded me just how hard the rest of the world works to get by, and confirmed that I was going to stick it out in med school, no matter what.

I was grateful when the second year began. At some point, I found my stride, and once again began to excel. By the end of the academic year I was feeling comfortable and looking forward to the next phase, which was referred to as the clinical years. Those in my class would no longer spend our days in lecture halls, and our evenings memorizing oceans of information. We would now spend all of our time in hospitals. These next two years had been like being dropped out of an airplane onto a foreign battlefield where you didn't know anybody or anything, and everyone else there knew it. We had landed safely, but we were definitely on foreign soil.

To make sure that we didn't forget our lowly status, we were made to wear these short little white coats. The garment itself seemed to say—*Yes, I want to be a doctor, but I'm not a doctor. I'm a clueless and silly kid who doesn't really know much of anything about the real world of medicine.* The distinctive short coat elicited suspicion from the patients who didn't appreciate being part of your education. It also gave the green light to anyone above your status to treat you like a dog. Nurses, pharmacists, security guards; they could all be rude and disdainful toward us without cause or consequence.

The hierarchy was as such: The highest position was the chairperson of whatever department the student was rotating through, such as surgery, internal medicine, obstetrics, emergency medicine, or pediatrics. Next in line was the attending physician who led the team of residents and students on the wards, or in the operating room. Next came the resident (in training) physicians whose status depended on their years completed in residency. Some residencies, like cardiothoracic surgery, were seven or eight years. Anesthesia was three years, internal medicine four years, general surgery five or six years. Next came every other person or patient or living creature in the building, before coming to the fourth-year medical student, who in their little white coat, was still above the third-year medical student like me, who had just dropped out of the sky onto the battlefield.

This was the transition that really separated us. This was what we had been working for from day one. For some entering the hospital was exciting; for others terrifying. For the rest it was simply disillusioning. You either loved and embraced it and thus excelled, or it shook you and brought you to your knees. Of course there were survivors who didn't dig it but figured out how to gut it out. That was me.

I hated the pomp and hierarchy—the arbitrary right to treat other people (other doctors, nurses, students, and even patients) like crap. I couldn't understand any of it really. I had been that young sick kid who needed help from people like these. Now I was trying to become one of them, and finding out that maybe I shouldn't be. The place was like a movie set, or a cruise ship, separated from reality and the rest of the world. The problem with that is that there were real people here, sick, and some of them dying.

Looking back, that period in my training reminded me of the 1972 movie *The Poseidon Adventure*. A luxury cruise ship is capsized by a rogue wave. The passengers band together into different clans, each group trying to survive and find a way out. People tend to find the natural order of things, the hierarchy, their clan. There are leaders and followers, rebels and martyrs and egomaniacs. There were some really good doctors teaching us. They were usually the quiet ones, sleep deprived and burned out. They believed in what they were doing in its most basic form. But there were many others who fit into one of those lesser categories. If you were lucky, you'd relate to any one of those types. If you were unlucky, you'd stand there with your mouth open in disbelief convinced you weren't going to last long.

    I couldn't relate to any of those in the hierarchy. They seemed to be missing the point, missing the obvious. It seemed to me that doctors existed to do the highest service—God's work—but they were missing that. It was a power struggle and political battle, and at times even a fist fight, but very rarely was it God's work. I found myself, instead, relating to the patients. I would double back to patients' rooms to sit and talk with them. It made us both feel better. They often reminded me of people in my family or people that I grew up with. They were normal, and I needed some of that. I did have duties though, and eventually I would return to the halls, to the end of the line of the passengers, all trying to climb that ladder and find an escape route from that capsized ship. Each of us had different disasters to escape from, and each had a unique motivation that led us to these halls.

CHAPTER 9
Blue Train

Coltrane's second album and its title track, "Blue Train," recorded in 1957. He was coming off a self-imposed detox from alcohol and heroin addiction after being kicked out of The Miles Davis Quintet for these vices. He is fresh as a daisy here and delivers his newfound signature sound, those sheets of sound, like rain pouring down a windowpane. Lee Morgan's trumpet, Curtis Fuller's trombone, and the rhythm section provide brief but sharp and beautiful respite between the downpours.

FROM DETECTIVE ROMAN'S *interview notes with various clinic staff:*

A few days later he was called into the clinic director's office. The director had been his proctor, and I don't think that the doctor really cared for him. The proctor is in charge of training the fellows—not necessarily training them how to be surgeons, because they were usually quite experienced. He was in charge of training them how to do liposuction and how to maximize profits. I think that the doctor resented the way that he had been treated by the proctor during those months of training—like he was a child or a novice. After all, the surgeon actually had more experience than the proctor. This resentment made things a little strange and uncomfortable between them.

I had intended to be a plastic surgeon at the beginning of all of this. Two years of four-to-six-week rotations through every area of medicine had taught me a couple of things. First, I no longer wanted to become a plastic surgeon, and second, I wasn't sure that I wanted to be a doctor at all. None of the specialties seemed right for me. Radiologists spent their days in dark rooms pouring over films from all areas of the body. Obstetrics and gynecology doctors spent their careers examining women's reproductive plumbing and delivering slippery babies. Pediatricians then had to deal with these anxious children and their even more anxious parents. Internists and family practice physicians formed the backbone of medicine as far as I was concerned, but the long term and chronic nature of their doctor-patient relationships just wasn't for me. I was interested in something of a more limited interaction. This would be best found, perhaps, in the surgical arena. In that world there were anesthesiologists, whose talents were focused mostly at the beginning and end of every surgery, and they had to spend too much of their days sitting and waiting for a surgeon to finish operating before going on to the next, and the next. Perhaps one of the surgical specialties would be a good fit.

My rotations as a medical student on the general surgery service and the vascular surgery service were particularly rough. As students, we were the lowest in that hierarchy and were made to do medical rounds on the patients before sunrise so that we would have all of the pertinent facts. The rounding was led by low-level surgical residents who would then present all of the summarized patient information to the chief resident who would then present to the attending surgeon. These crack-of-dawn rounds were not only tough on us, but also disorienting to the patients who were awakened at 5:00 a.m. by a room full of strangers wanting to ask questions and palpate their bodies.

After a long day of retractor holding in the operating room, there was a second round of rounding, usually as the sun was setting, or long after dark. This time it was with the attending surgeon. The attending surgeon would usually patronize the patients and humiliate the residents. I recall one of these attendings announcing to the group of us students. "Residents are like rugs," he had said. "They were meant to be walked on daily, and to be beaten once a week." The abuse was indiscriminate and often ran uphill.

Us lowliest of medical students were meant to learn by watching the destruction of our superiors by someone even more superior. As I have mentioned before, sometimes those who are abused become abusers themselves. Many of us residents and students would someday become intimidators and abusers as we scaled the surgical hierarchy. Not me. I always hated that dynamic and believed that it was the worst way to learn. Even so, we all learned.

Weeks spent on other surgical specialties were sometimes better. I remember that ENT (ear nose and throat) was much more civilized, but I could never convince myself that I would be able endure a career that involved operating in tiny spaces like ears or noses or throats. Neurosurgery was fascinating, but the results of brain surgery for tumors or aneurysms or trauma were often unpredictable, and outcomes seemed like a roll of the dice.

Plastic surgery still appealed to me, but enduring five or six years of surgery training before I even begin my real plastic surgery training seemed off putting. So did the idea of lingering for years in the cosmetic world of tummy tucks and breast implants before getting an opportunity to do the type of reconstructive work that I had seen on the television years before. I was lost and wondering if medical school had been a big mistake. I recall crying on my girlfriend's shoulder that night when I finally acknowledged my fears—that I had wasted eight years of education.

Meanwhile, my dear friend Gabriel had spent the last four years finishing up his undergraduate degree and taking the medical school entrance exam, but he had not succeeded in gaining acceptance. He was planning on retaking the exam and re-applying. He needed a pep talk, so we decided to hang out one night. We went to one of our favorite spots, one we hadn't been to in a while.

WHEN I WAS growing up, there was a nearby train track that serviced freight trains and passenger trains. This particular stretch was infamous to us kids. It passed through a field that was bordered by residential neighborhoods on both sides. Children often played in that field or crossed the tracks on their way to or from school, or to meet friends. I knew one boy my age who had been killed by a train accidentally and another who had committed suicide there. There was a section that passed under a high freeway overpass. You could jump up on the concrete base of the overpass supports and drink beer, or smoke cigarettes, or make out with a girl. I could play my saxophone there, and nobody would hear or care. The place had a sad and spooky vibe. I liked to lay coins on the tracks. We'd gather up the flattened coins and leave them as a gift to the dead, to those that had died on those tracks. The coins were always gone the next time we'd come.

As I said, Gabriel and I were fanatics in our love of jazz. It was one of the things that made us so close. We'd do this thing where we would pick a jazz track and describe what was going on in the music, what the artists were trying to communicate to the listener. Sometimes one of us would nod his head in cool agreement and say, "exactly man." Other times we would burst out laughing at the others' messed up interpretation. I brought a little handheld tape recorder that had a crappy little speaker. I used it in my car because the car's radio was broken. We listened to a cassette recording of John Coltrane's studio album *Blue Train* that evening at the train tracks while we discussed Gabriel's options and my career path.

"I don't know Gabriel. I think I fucked up."

"What? Why do you say that?"

"I'm not feeling it man. I'm not sure what to do. I've invested so much time and energy into this, but it doesn't feel right. I get physically ill every morning on the way into the hospital, and I can't wait to get home at night. Voices of rage are in my head when I have to sit by silently and listen to these pompous attendings pimp the residents with questions and humiliate them when they don't know the answers. I don't know if I can do that next year. I might just lose it and strangle one of those fuckers."

I was on my back looking up at the rats crawling around overhead in the freeway supports. Gabriel had hopped down and was lying on his side with his head on one of the rails.

"What are you talking about? I'd give anything to be where you are," Gabriel admonished. "You have to just keep going. Don't ever stop. Just get through the day. You might find that things look totally different tomorrow, or maybe the day after that. Just keep going."

We lay there silently for a while contemplating our fates until Gabriel said, "I can hear one coming. I can't tell from which direction, and it's far off, but it's coming. Toss me a coin."

CHAPTER 10
A Love Supreme, Acknowledgment

A Love Supreme, John Coltrane, 1965. This track, "Part I Acknowledgement" 7:42. Coltrane feared that God had taken his ability to play music as punishment for his addiction to alcohol and heroin. He bargained with God. *"Give me back my gift and I will preach through this horn for you."* I had always thought that the album title was about a man's love for a woman, but he's referring to God's love for us. Imagine how supreme that kind of love is. The bass and piano lead you into the church, and Coltrane shuts the door. I feel a tug a war in his sax, a back and forth, and back and forth, with the rhythm section like the parishioners and the choir chanting while Coltrane is speaking in tongues; finally, a surrender.

From Detective Roman's *interview notes with liposuction nurse:*
A few days after his meeting with the proctor he disappeared again. The nurses couldn't find him. They had a patient on the table ready to go. They looked around everywhere, but they couldn't find him. Finally, they found the doctor in the prep room. He liked that room because the sterilizing autoclave was in there and it kept the little room warm. The nurse knocked and there was no answer. She entered

and found the doctor on his knees. His eyes closed, murmuring. She thought that he was praying.

I WAS SICK of Detective Roman's interrogation and Dr. Sander observing me as if I was an endangered species. I didn't want to talk about my past; it was exhausting and sometimes painful. I was here to heal, not to hurt.

"Can we table this probing for a while, Dr. Sanders? It's draining, and, frankly, I fail to see how dredging up the past helps. In fact, I think it's impeding my progress."

She looked at my eyes for a long while, like straight into my head, ignoring my plea to stop the inquisition.

"We are making progress whether you recognize it or not, Michael. There are areas we need to explore, among them, religion. You've mentioned religion and God quite often. Do you consider yourself a religious man?" she asked finally.

"There is no short answer. It should be known, or at least clarified, that I believe in a God, but I have no idea what God is. I know that in the darkest moments, I am pulled out. I am rescued. I don't know why. I don't depend on it. It only happens when I am truly at the end of options, at least in my head, when I am desperate, when I am on the verge. Then is when it happens.

Why doesn't it happen the same for everyone? Why do the things that happen, happen? For me they just do. I am pulled out of despair, perhaps temporarily, but I take note. I bargain, I pray, but I never really know. So much time passes that I convince myself that it was all in my mind, my imagination, then it happens again; I am saved. It happens like that for me over and over and over and I tell myself that I don't deserve this love. I am being helped by God for a reason, but I don't know what that reason is. It doesn't matter what I do, it doesn't ever seem worthy of that love.

Why did you save me when I was young and ill? Why did you put me in that wretched school and in those awful jobs? Why did you break my heart so many times? Why did you blacken my eye? Why did you teach me to succeed and to beat the odds? Am I accruing a debt that I must repay? It must be so. I will someday become aware of my calling, and I will have my opportunity to repay the kindness and supreme love. Until then, I am blind, feeling my way along a wall, entering doorways that lead to rooms that lead to nowhere."

There was a long silence after my diatribe. Then the doctor paged through papers she had in a folder. She handed a few sheets to me. They were handwritten.

"Your wife has given us some of your writings, some things that she thought might be helpful for us, as we try to help you. Did you write this?' she asked. I looked it over and quickly recognized it.

"She's my ex-wife, you know. No. That's Gabriel's stuff." I read it slowly to myself:

God, if There Is One

Morning brought clarity
The pain in my head was gone

I stood and shuffled a little to convince myself
then sat and stared off considering the possibility

I know what this is
This time I recognize it

It has me now, though I can't quite remember when that happened
Small, unnoticed changes over days and weeks and months?
Or was it a light switch?
Neither

When the panic came it was not like a punch
in the face or a slow moving fog. It came
as an ocean does, with weight and intention insurmountable, rolling
      over me

Once this has you it always does
Nobody goes un-mad. You don't ever find your mind
once you've lost it
Rather, it swirls. Breath is faster. Weight is crushing

I am calling to you

Jesus
Mary
God and the angels
Please do not abandon me here. Don't bring me here
only to leave me. This burden will surely break me

The calm of exhaustion eventually follows, and I feel the change
The waters recede
I sleep

When I wake, there is a moment when it is all as before
coffee and plans and memories. Still
it soon creeps back in

The voices are constant
They direct me

Things are clear now

I know that Jesus saves. The billboards
confirm that

Let the doctors laugh. Don't they realize
he is the original Savior
These doctors are just weak effort — fools
puppets laughing at their master

The pills that they gave me were the opposite of medicine
more like glue or syrup, they coated my mind and slowed it

Now my thoughts are clear

I was in the cemetery this morning. I spoke
with my relatives, my ancestors
They will wait there for me
They know

I have much to do first
The woman that I love has been sleeping with my friends
My friends have been plotting my demise. There are things they know

You see, I have done it all, and tried it all
yet they remain. This world does not want me

The voices do not comfort me. Instead, they stir me
like a boiling mess
Though I do what they bid me they do not relent

The ones I love no longer know me
They fear me now, and I no longer remember why
I love them

This I know
A train can take the coin that lies upon the track
crush it into copper and bring its luster back

Lay you then upon that rail and feel the cold steel rattle
You are damaged, twisted, busted. You have lost the battle

Bow then to the ocean to the moon and to the sun
for tomorrow you will be with him
God, if there is one

CHAPTER 11
Crepuscule With Nellie

Thelonius Sphere Monk. "Crepuscule with Nellie," 2:45 The 1963 album *Criss-Cross* on the Columbia label. Dissonant and sparse harmonies—the trademark of perhaps the most unique musician in the history of jazz. "There are no wrong notes," he once said about his style. Indeed. something is never wrong with Monk's play, its right, so strange and beautiful. Charlie Rouse and his saxophone layer on the top of it like a shadow. Crepuscule—dusk, partial darkness, fireflies, and crickets, but also spirits and demons.

***

From Detective Roman's interviews with two liposuction clinical nurses and other staff:

The staff was growing worried about the doctor, even the proctor. His behavior had become more erratic, lacking the charm he normally exhibited. The staff said that the doctor was really good, technically good, but it wasn't only that. The patients really loved him. The other doctors were very artificial, using the same rehearsed lines and instructions, and jokes, but he, he had a way of connecting with the patients in a sincere way that they really appreciated. He would listen to them. Usually, if the patient was in pain or apprehensive during the procedure, nurses would have them squeeze a ball or their hand and try to relax them. It was effective, a little, but the doctor could say a few words or maybe put his hand on their shoulder, and they would calm down. But lately he seemed like he was the one who really needed some help. He needed someone to put their hand on his shoulder.

DESPITE MY WEARINESS, interviewing continued, coming at me in waves.

"Have you ever been a violent man, doctor?" Detective Roman asked. "Have you felt like lashing out, getting some sort of revenge?" Dr. Sanders and I looked at each other, not really knowing what the detective was implying.

"Violence sickens me." I responded. "Does that answer your question?"

"Aren't you cutting people when you do surgery? Isn't operating a sort of controlled assault? I mean why *did* you become a surgeon? Why not an internist, or a psychiatrist like Doc Sanders here?"

Doctor Sanders looked shocked. "Don't answer him." she said. "Just keep on with your story. I think that the detective will find his answers if he just listens a little."

"Fine," Roman relented. "Then how about you share a bit more about you pal Gabriel?"

I rolled my eyes and settled in, calmly relaying another sliver of my past and that of my closest friend.

WHILE GABRIEL WAS re-applying himself, I had been in damage-control mode. During my fourth year of medical school in Milwaukee, Gabriel had gained acceptance to a medical school in Washington, D.C. While he was finishing his inaugural year, I was soul-searching. I had failed to identify an area of medicine that I felt compelling enough to spend the rest of my days practicing. As a medical student, when you don't know what you want to do, it's like missing a train—you don't do the externship, you don't get the letters of recommendation, and on match day, you don't match.

I told the detective that *matching* is the term used to describe what happens toward the end of medical school, when the graduating students are matched to a residency program in the field that he or she has chosen to pursue. The student applies to programs throughout the country. Some of the programs offer interviews to the student. The student enters a ranking of the programs that they have interviewed at, and the programs enter a ranking of all of the students that they have interviewed. It all gets plugged into a national database and *voila*, on match day you've matched with an institution that ranked you high, as well. Upon graduation, everyone is notified as to where each of their fellow students will be continuing their training and education.

Failing to land a match was humiliating, and I tried to convince myself that it wasn't. I reminded myself that all it really meant was that I was undecided, and that there's really no shame in that. Although true, my rationalization did little to make me feel any better. I think that it was a surprise to everyone that I went unclaimed. I imagined my classmates wondering what had happened.

My fellow students were quite focused and decided. They were in a different gear, and I was spinning my wheels. Even so, I had an *MD* after my name now, and I needed to find work as a doctor. I scrambled to find a one-year position at an academic program in Chicago that would afford me an additional year of rotations and hopefully help me to decide my field of practice. This was called a surgical preliminary year. I would be a doctor, functioning as surgical intern on multiple different surgical services, each for six-week intervals. These different services included ENT, neurosurgery, trauma surgery, pediatric surgery, vascular surgery, and a lot of general surgery. I was paid an entry-level salary and was basically cheap labor for the hospital. In contrast to the preliminary program, the categorical general surgery training program at this hospital had five residents per year. These residents would go on from year one to year five, likely with a year of research thrown in, to make it six years of training. The graduate, having finished the training, would then go on to start a practice somewhere. This is not what I was doing. Me and nineteen other undecided, confused souls had signed a one-year contract to work for the hospital without any real expectation that there would be anything after that. It was a marriage of convenience—the hospital got its cheap labor, and the preliminary intern gained experience and letters of recommendation that would, ostensibly, propel him to a categorical position at this institution or another, beginning the following year. It was a bit of a gamble, but I was hopeful that once I had an opportunity to prove myself, it would all work out.

I didn't realize it at first, but I had wandered through the gates of hell. A *malignant program* is a term used to describe a training facility known for its brutal treatment of the surgeons in training. This Chicago hospital was in that dubious club. I didn't discover this until I was already there. Years later, when I would tell other surgeons where I had done my internship their eyes would widen and they might raise an eyebrow, as if to say "Oh really? So how was that?"

"Yes, how was that?" the detective interjected.

"Ugly," I responded.

We began our first year of training on July 1. It was unfortunately close to the Fourth of July holiday, especially if you are on your fourth day of being a doctor and you are the intern surgeon on the trauma service of a busy Chicago trauma center.

The Fourth weekend in Chicago is an occasion for explosives, and often an opportunity for people to shoot each other, or to drive intoxicated and crash at high speeds into other drivers, or pedestrians, or immovable concrete and steel structures. During that chaotic weekend, I was put into an ambulance with a critical patient needing to be transported across the campus for a radiology exam. I remember the chief resident putting four syringes into the chest pocket of my white coat. He said, "If this happens give him this one. If this happens give this. If this happens give this one, and if this happens give that." The door closed, and I looked at the patient being bag ventilated by the EMT who I'm sure knew what he was doing more than me. I remember thinking, *Please don't let this, this, this, or that happen because I had forgotten what each syringe was and which to give for what.*

As weeks passed, I was assigned to the neurosurgery rotation. It was a mix of adult and pediatric patients with tumors, trauma, aneurysms... etc. Neurosurgery was fascinating stuff—operating on the brain. Unfortunately, surgical outcomes were unpredictable. For instance, a patient would come in with a cerebral hemorrhage from a ruptured brain aneurysm. They would be unconscious. The surgeon would remove part of the skull, clip the bleeding vessel, remove the blood, and replace the bone and suture the scalp incision. The patient would often progress well for a few days but then suddenly deteriorate due delayed cerebral edema, which is swelling of the brain. A coma would ensue, followed by brain death, which is what happens when the pressure inside the skull is too high to allow adequate blood flow to the brain.

There was an unusual second year neurosurgery resident—Steven L. Dendloffer. He was from Boston and had graduated from Harvard Medical School. He was quirky and extremely intelligent. He was only one year older than me but seemed to be from my father's generation. He wore a fedora hat and a raincoat to work every day, like some old guy from the 1940s. His manner of speaking was peculiar, as he often referred to himself in the third person, always including his full name when he did so—"Steven L. Dendloffer, MD." I had found him fascinating, and I followed him around the wards helping with the daily tasks until he would be called off to the operating room. Like most who are different, he was brutally ridiculed by his fellow residents and even by the staff neurosurgeons. They would try to catch any mistake or misspoken word and then all laugh at him when he presented patients during evening rounds. He would get visibly flustered but would carry on undeterred. He would never speak about or acknowledge this mistreatment.

One afternoon, a toddler was brought into our ER after a car accident. The child had been in a car seat, facing forward in the back seat. Her mother was driving and crested a hill, only to find a dump truck stopped immediately on the descent. She collided with the back of the truck, and somehow the car seat lunged forward, and the child's head struck the back of the front seat. The child was acting disoriented but was conscious. I remember looking down at her on the gurney. She was awake and calm, maybe too calm for a toddler. She had a bruise on her forehead, but no other signs of trauma. Within an hour she deteriorated, losing consciousness, and requiring intubation and mechanical ventilation. Her brain was swelling. Despite all medical interventions, we were unable to reverse this process. Days later, she lay in the pediatric ICU, brain dead. The neurosurgery staff surgeon had explained the grave prognosis to the mother, who was understandably in denial and not yet ready to authorize the withdrawal of mechanical support; doing so would result in the child's death, as her breathing mechanisms were no longer functioning—the result of the profound brain damage.

Dr. Dendloffer and I stood outside the large window looking into the child's room. He explained to me that he just didn't have it in him to face the mother again. He told me to go in and talk to her. He was my superior, and I did as I was told. I don't remember exactly what I said to her, but I do remember her dropping to her knees and wrapping her arms around my legs, crying, and begging me to save her daughter. I remember telling her that in a way her daughter was already dead. The words sounded so harsh when I heard myself saying them, and I immediately wished that I hadn't. I thought that those words might help her grasp the scientific certainty of what had happened, but I was wrong.

The hospital had a skywalk that separated the building in which the ICU was located from the rest of the main hospital. I walked out to the middle of it and looked eastward at the Chicago skyline in the distance. It was dusk and the buildings were reflecting the red and orange light of the sun setting in the west. I thought about all of the people out there that were unaware of what had just happened. I wished that I could be one of them, but it was too late. I would never again be one of them. I have always regretted how direct I was with that woman that day, and I have always resented being put in that situation. I had been a doctor for only three months. Now I truly was learning the hard way.

Of course, the child died. Later I heard gossip that Dr. Dendloffer was going to be fired from the neurosurgery program due to his poor performance. He was so smart, but like many extremely intelligent people, he lacked social and interpersonal skills. At the end of the month I moved on to a different surgical service. I learned months later that Dr. Steven L. Dendloffer was dead. He had hung himself."

CHAPTER 12
II B.S.

"II B.S." 1963, from the album *Mingus Mingus Mingus Mingus Mingus*. It's an upbeat version of "Haitian Fight Song." The bass of Charles Mingus is the star for sure, but after that solo intro, it busts into a party to end all parties, like a storm before a hurricane.

FROM DETECTIVE ROMAN'S *interview notes with a liposuction nurse:*

That day the nurse had witnessed him praying, he simply stood up and apologized, then did the procedure. The nurse was not sure what the doctor and the proctor had spoken about that day in the proctor's office. The nurse wanted to respect the doctor's confidentially, but she really needed some direction here. The next time that she saw the proctor she told him about what she had witnessed. He said that there was no crime in praying, but that he too was noticing strange behaviors and had brought them up to the doctor in private that day. The doctor again apologized, and they parted ways. The proctor asked the nurse to keep an eye on things and report to him, especially if there were any instances that posed a risk of harm to any of them or to the patients.

Dr. Sanders and Detective Roman seemed more interested in my personal connection to Gabriel than our professional tribulations. I told them about a weekend Gabriel had visited while I was living in Cicero—a tough area in West Chicago.

We had gone to our favorite jazz place—The Green Mill. After that, we went to some dance clubs. We ended up frustrated and doubled back to my apartment to pick up my sax. I drove us to a place on the others side of the Eisenhower Freeway, behind a warehouse, where a railroad track passed by. It was the perfect place to practice, especially if you weren't any good. It was almost as good as our spot in Milwaukee under the freeway. The sounds would echo off of the warehouse, and the trains going by were awful. There was constant noise from the freeway. The people living nearby were used to the racket, and they couldn't care less.

When I played there, Gabriel would squat on his haunches and listen. I tried to get him to give it a go—to try the horn—but he was content to listen to me, and to the orchestra of chaos around us. The dance clubs had been a bust. Guys like us weren't meant to pick up strange girls at clubs. No, we were the messed-up loners playing saxophone between a warehouse and the train tracks, with nobody around to listen. I loved playing, but I would rather have been the guy in the club who had the look, and the friends, and the girls. Playing sax on dark streets may to some sound sexy and hip, but it wasn't. It was lonely and sad and pathetic.

Gabriel had spent that night in my Cicero apartment. We got home before dawn. We didn't talk much the next day, and he left to head back to D.C. I never picked up that sax again.

My story veered back to my job, and Dr. Sanders and the detective indulged my ramblings without interruption. I told them about my next rotations, which all had glimpses of insanity. I was doing several months of general surgery rotations at different hospitals in the Chicago area which were also associated with the training program. There were five categorical residents in the general surgery residency program. These were the ones with the five-year contract and the guaranteed future. I was not one of those. I was with a one-year cheap labor cohort, all of us medical misfits of sorts who were left unclaimed like ugly dogs in a pound. The others tended to look down on those of us who had been undecided and unmatched. We were, in a way, nothing more than one-year temps.

I would often look at those burgeoning surgeons and their supervisors with envy and wonder what was it that they had that I did not. What ingredient of success was missing in me? They appeared happy, confident, like they were set for life. We misfits on the other hand were simply workers. We were ordered around and humiliated, and there was really no effort made to train us—to teach us. The categorical residents were part of the brotherhood. Sure, they were ordered around and humiliated as well, but they were being trained and taught a craft. I, on the other hand, was winging it, trying to learn as much as I could, hoping to maybe impress someone along the way so that I could get into a categorical position, in something surgical. Although we all tried to appear unfazed by it, the malignant nature of this specific place was beginning to take its toll on all of us, even the chosen.

During those months, from time to time, a categorical resident would quit. One by one, they were quitting. I was never told why, but each time one of them left, I'd get called into the program director's office. He had his own secretary who would lead me into his office and announce me by name. The director had no idea who any of us in the one-year program were. He was a vascular surgeon with a particularly caustic personality. Perhaps you become mean and sadistic when your business is doing surgeries to reroute blood flow in order to save rotten toes and limbs, but only to inevitably have to amputate them because the procedures had failed.

The director had light blue eyes that seemed unnaturally bright, like they were not real. Everything about him made me uncomfortable. I sat across from him as he sat behind a huge wooden desk. He didn't tell me why, but he said that I would be leaving the cushy plastic surgery rotation, or the chill urology month to go on to something more interesting or more appropriate. I knew what that meant, and I knew that I was replacing a resident who had just quit, and I knew that I would be going to the very rotation that had been so horrible that it caused the resident to choose an entirely different career rather than endure it any longer.

"I'm happy to help sir in any way you need me," I said.

One might think that maybe it was a rare occurrence, but this sudden departure occurred three times during the first half of my intern year. Each time, I was told to replace the departing resident. I was "preliminary," a mere substitute, a warm body to fill a space. There was no consideration given to my aspirations. Each time, I headed into battle with a chip on my shoulder, but one that I kept carefully hidden under my long white resident's coat.

I worked very hard with the intention of showing everyone that I could be, and should be, accepted into the six-year general surgery program, perhaps into the very spot vacated by the last to depart. I took it as a personal challenge to succeed where the chosen ones had failed. Each time that I completed one of those tough rotations, my confidence would grow. I was beginning to believe that I could, in fact, do this. I certainly did impress the chief residents whose job it was to steer the ship and delegate the work required, until the next green bunch rotated through. Some came to regard me as someone who was tough, but also smart and dependable. I was quiet and respectful, and always did as I was told.

As the year progressed, I was called once again to the program director's office. This time, however, it was for a required check-in. Part of the program director's job was to meet with each of the preliminary residents toward the end of their intern year to discuss their performance, and to counsel them on a career path. By this point I had been working fourteen-hour shifts, alternating with thirty-six-hour shifts for months. Like all of us interns, I was barely awake at any given time.

As I sat across from the director, I noticed the photos on that big hardwood desk. I assumed that they were his daughters. The frames were turned in a way that he could see them, but so too could the person sitting across from him. Both girls were quite beautiful, with big smiles, and long flowing blonde hair. They had the same eyes as him. They appeared to be roughly my age. I remember thinking how odd it was that these surgeons actually had wives and children—people who loved them. They were so intimidating and awful to us, but they must be just like regular people around their families, or so I surmised.

I must have been staring at those photos and thinking those thoughts for some time when I noticed that the director wasn't speaking. My gaze slowly shifted from the pictures to his scowling face.

"Are you getting laid enough son?" he asked.

I was shocked by the question. I couldn't tell him what I was actually thinking right then. Although I had been staring at the photos of his daughters, it was more of a daydream, I was so sleep deprived that sex was the last thing on my mind... until he mentioned it, of course.

"Is that ever possible sir?" I replied, trying to be funny.

He didn't smile.

"Are you having a good time here with us?"

"Yes sir. I am. I really appreciate the opportunity you've given me. I've decided that I want to continue on in general surgery... as a career, I mean."

"Is that so? Have you any idea where you'd like to do this?"

"I was quite hoping that I might continue on here, sir."

"Were you?"

"Why yes, sir. The program is down three out its original five categorical residents because they've quit. I've been able to perform in conditions they could not. I would seem like a natural choice, sir."

At least he seemed to consider it for a few seconds.

"Our policy is to not accept our preliminary residents into the categorical residency program here."

I was shocked. I would never have imagined that. I had been working so hard to make an impression—to get one of those coveted spots.

"That seems rather arbitrary," I said. "I mean, what will you do to fill the spots then?"

Again he paused, and maybe he even seemed to feel a little empathy. He quickly brushed that aside.

"That's not your concern."

"You see, but it is my concern. I've earned the opportunity. It's very much my concern, sir."

"We'll write you very good letters of recommendation. Start looking into programs and we'll do our part. That's it. You can go."

That was it. If a zombie can be any more of a zombie, could the undead be any more undead? That was me from that point on—the walking dead.

I continued to perform my duties with professionalism, but my heart was no longer in it. I was going through the paces, marking time. I did start looking into programs to apply to. This time I'd have an advantage. Now I knew what I wanted to do, and what I was good at. I wanted to help the sick people, like desperate sick ones. It would require surgery, the kind most other doctors didn't want to deal with. I would specialize in what most couldn't handle. That seemed to be my strength. I had found my place.

"That was a big breakthrough for you, wasn't it," Dr. Sanders asked.

"Did you celebrate?" the detective added. "Did you share your news?"

That evening I had received a call from Gabriel. I was cheerful and ready to share my decision, until he told me that he was failing his exams in medical school. He told me that the professors were giving the answers to the other students, giving them some sort of advantage over him.

The intern year in Chicago had changed me. I had developed the ability to cut to the meat of the issue. I didn't have much patience for my friend. Gabriel's excuses sounded like a copout to me. All that I really could do was try to motivate him to stop making excuses, and to stop blaming others for his failures, and to do whatever it took to turn things around. The conversation frustrated me. It left me with a bad feeling—Gabriel wouldn't make it.

CHAPTER 13
Solitude

"Solitude" by Duke Ellington, 4:40. It's from the 1958 album *Ellington Indigos*. He made many recordings of this tune, which was written by Duke himself, but this is the one. It was the opening theme for Ron Cuzner's midnight jazz radio show on WFMR—*The Dark Side*. The beginning is such soft solo piano that you don't even hear it at first. Typically, the orchestra would play early in the tune, but not this version—just Duke. Even Ron wouldn't say anything. At 1:15 into it there's a taunting tapping of the keys. At 1:42 the snare joins in and the power of the playing ramps up, then the orchestra comes in. That's when Ron Cuzner's distinctive voice would welcome me to the dark side of whatever day of the week it was.

FROM DETECTIVE ROMAN'S interviews with the proctor:

The proctor convinced him to take some time off. He returned a couple of weeks later and seemed like he had been energized, refreshed. Unfortunately, the surgeries that had to be postponed due to his unplanned vacation, now had to be added on every day until they were caught up. The company wasn't going to lose any money on his account. This increased workload quickly erased any benefit that vacation had given him. The proctor said he saw him shaking his hands all of the time, or wringing them—trying to get the feeling back.

There were some things I couldn't explain to Dr. Sanders. I didn't want her to start thinking that I was crazy, but all of this talking about my past was making me remember things that I had tried so hard to forget. The lonely times when there was nobody who could help me. No one knew of my distress and alienation because I hid it so well. It was at times like this, when I was confused or maybe a little blue, I would get sentimental, and I didn't want to show that side of myself to this cop or this shrink.

Although I was lonely, some things I remember fondly. I often think of those times when I'd be up studying college chemistry or history at home. When midnight came, my father, having finished his late dinner of broiled pork chops, would drift off on the couch. My mother would wander off to bed, and I'd be up reading, transcribing, memorizing in the corner of that room, with the solitary desk lamp, and the radio.

My dad would wake up and flip on Ron Cuzner's jazz show, *The Dark Side*. I'd take a break from my books and listen to the show for a while with my old man. I loved the introduction to the show—Duke Ellington's "Solitude." Very sparse solo piano played for several minutes, then a buildup, and finally a somewhat raucous ensemble, but it started out so slowly. That's what made it so beautiful. It builds. There are a thousand versions of that song by Duke Ellington, but that's the only one that I still hear in my head.

Dr. Sanders asks me about the significance of the song. "What does it represent to you, Michael?"

I think for a minute. "It is representative of that time in my life—the slow solitary buildup," I tell her.

I would wait for Ron's voice, and it would be there for me. He'd say, "Welcome to the dark side of Tuesday morning," or whatever morning it might be. Suddenly I was not alone anymore. My father was passed out again on the couch. My mother was snoring in her bedroom, and I was studying physics with Ron and The Duke.

Detective Roman seemed less than intrigued by my musical revelation. He eyed Dr. Sanders, as if asking her to yield the floor.

"Michael, you told us before that you and Gabriel similarly enjoyed listening to jazz together. Would you say that was a foundation of your relationship, just like with you and your dad?"

There were similarities, but, as I thought about it, I was to Gabriel as much a mentor and emotional guardian as my dad had been to me. Sometimes I even admonished him as my father had me.

I told Detective Roman how Gabriel had been sounding paranoid. He was accusatory and even claimed that his professors were trying to get him kicked out of medical school. He had all kinds of facts which he presented to me, all very complicated. What he was saying had just enough believability to it that I tried to give him the benefit of the doubt. As I had already told the detective, my father rarely tolerated excuses. He believed that things that happened to us were caused by us. I had projected that same outlook onto Gabriel, more than once, essentially scolding him for blaming his failings on others. It had finally come to a head when he whined about medical school, and I sternly told him to stop making excuses. I had no idea that we would not speak again for several years. I felt a sudden regret for my lack of empathy, and the meanness never before present, especially with my best friend.

There were reasons that I had become so impatient—so cold. I had been beaten, like a new recruit in boot camp. I was focused on what was happening in my life. I was finishing up my year in Chicago. I had secured a categorical position in general surgery in Pittsburgh. The position had only one catch—I would have to start over and repeat my intern year.

To most, that might sound horrible, but by then I felt as though I had walked across hot coals to get to where I was. I was relieved to have secured my future; my sacrifice had paid off. I was achieving my goal with no excuses. I would be the strongest intern there. It would be a fresh start. I had escaped Milwaukee and now I'd be getting out of Chicago. I proposed to my girlfriend, and we prepared to move.

FOR THE NEXT five years I was training in Pittsburgh for *my* life. There was no longer any question as to what I was going to do, who I was going to be. It was all surgery, all of the time. I would no longer be dabbling in neurosurgery, ENT, urology. Most of my rotations were general surgery, which involves intestinal surgeries for cancers, breast surgery for cancer, hernias, gallbladders, and appendicitis . . . etc. There were specialized months in transplant surgery and vascular surgery, burn surgery, and quite a bit of trauma surgery.

I excelled while in Pittsburgh. It was never easy, but I was welcomed into the program. I belonged there, and that made all the difference. I'd like to say that I was okay, that I had come through unscathed, but the truth is that the brutal hours and the stress that I had endured in Chicago and the five years that followed in Pittsburgh had done something to me. I had crossed over to somewhere. I wasn't sad or regretful, but I knew that there would be no turning back. The bridge was now gone.

On the one hand, I finally felt confident again. After so many years of feeling behind and incompetent, trying to catch up, or pretending to be something that I really wasn't, I had legitimately made it through. But there was another side to it all. It all had taken quite a toll on me.

"You seem proud of your achievement... of becoming a surgeon, Michael. Do you still feel that way," Dr. Sanders asked.

"There were consequences," I said. "There was a cost to it, a price that I think I am still paying."

CHAPTER 14
Imagination

"Imagination" by Chet Baker from the 1988 documentary about the trumpet player's life, *Let's Get Lost.* The James Dean of jazz, the natural trumpeter and soft throated vocalist lived longer than most junkies do. One of the architects of the cool style of West Coast Jazz, he succumbed to heroin addiction. Later in his career he swept floors in LA while he struggled to learn how to play and sing again after his teeth were broken so badly by a drug dealer's gang that he had to have them all pulled. In this version from the movie soundtrack, he mumbles through a broken mouth to pay homage to the one thing that may still be able to pull him out of the pain and into a dream, not heroin, imagination. In much of the later footage he appears much older than his fifty-eight years. Not long after the filming, his long dream would end on a sidewalk beneath a third-floor hotel room in Amsterdam.

WE HAD ENDED our session on the previous day early, allowing me to rest and process all that I had revealed. The next morning we were at it again, with Detective Roman's familiar refrain.

"The stuff about you accomplishing your goals is good information, Doc. But I'd like to steer the conversation back again to Gabriel."

"Sorry detective, but please don't call me Doc. I prefer Michael. Doc makes me feel uncomfortable. You see, I'm not overly impressed with myself for being a doctor. There's not a thing about me—no credit cards, address labels, not even my driver's license—that has *Dr.* or *MD* on it. Fuck that. Why should I consider myself to be different than anybody else?"

"Okay then, Michael it is," said Detective Roman, seemingly unphased. "One more thing, Michael, we understand that you both liked music, that your dad liked it. So, no need to rehash that. Okay?"

Dr. Sanders turned her head and glared at the detective. Her demeanor throughout the past few days had been opposite of the detective's. Where he was bold and pushy, she was very quiet and thoughtful. I found that to be quite a contrast to the doctors I had been around all of my life. She was the type that made it look as though she was in the back seat, but she was actually in the driver's seat. She always directed the interviews, even when the detective thought that he was asking the questions. This time she disagreed with the detective.

"Sorry to interrupt, Detective Roman, but music has been an important aspect of Michael's relationships. It's relevant."

"Thank you, Dr. Sanders. Shall I continue?" I asked with a hint of sarcasm.

"Please do," she said with a sly smile. "Detective Roman and I would like to hear more about how you and Gabriel became estranged, and why."

"That's right," the detective said. "So you didn't see this good friend Gabe of yours for years? Not even a phone call?"

"His name is Gabriel, not Gabe," I huffed. "And as for not seeing him, well, you see, I was so focused on my training, I'm ashamed to say that I didn't give Gabriel much thought for a long while."

Initially, I had kept waiting for him to call me again, but he didn't. It was like a breakup. A year passed, then another. In time, I became more okay with the whole thing. I would come home to Milwaukee from Pittsburgh for holidays if I got the time off. I was in the hospital one hundred-and-twenty hours per week for those five years, but we did get some holidays. Even when I did go home, I never reached out to Gabriel. I suppose that I didn't really want to know what was going on with him... I didn't want to hear excuses for his failures. Plus, I resented him for not staying in touch, either. I had hoped that he continued on in medical school and was succeeding, but the continued silence gave me a bad feeling, and I tried not to think about it.

Despite my intentions, he was always in my mind. I began to think more and more about Gabriel. I recall one day having an alarming thought. It occurred to me that maybe there was something wrong with Gabriel. Maybe he was mentally ill. Could that explain his behavior? Suddenly it all started to make sense—his paranoia, maybe he was having delusions. I had been so caught up in my own life that I hadn't realized it. Here I was, a doctor, and I had totally missed the warning signs. Only years later did this finally occur to me, while I was sitting at my desk studying, and thinking about Gabriel.

I still had his mother's phone number, so I gathered the courage to call her. She was reluctant at first to tell me much, but when I expressed my concern, she opened up. I was right, he was suffering from some sort of mental breakdown and had been hospitalized. She told me that it had really gotten bad after he went back to Peru. Relatives there had to have him hospitalized and sent back to the States eventually. They said he was delusional and depressed. I felt like a fool for not realizing this sooner.

A couple of months after that visit I did see Gabriel again, when I came home for my father's funeral. I had received a call from my mother telling me that my father had died unexpectedly. I was in my fifth year in the surgical program and was the chief resident of the trauma service at the time.

Instead of going home to grieve with my family, I stayed in Pittsburgh until I had to go back for the funeral service, which had been delayed a week. I kept coming to work every day like nothing had changed. One of my fellow residents must have told the supervising surgeon that my father had passed. He said to me one morning, "What are you doing here Michael? You know you're in shock, right? That's the first stage of grieving—denial. Get out of here. Go and be with your family."

I was in shock, or more like a trance. The relationship with my father had been estranged since I had moved out of the family home. When I started residency in Pittsburgh, I was so busy that we hardly spoke, and he had become increasingly depressed and withdrawn. We didn't have a falling out; we just drifted apart as my life was so focused on my training.

When I was told that he had died, my first thought was relief, not for me, but for him. I was glad that he didn't have to suffer any longer. It took a long time for the permanence of his death to sink into my brain, and the realization that I would never have the chance to reconnect with my father and re-establish our bond. I was mature enough finally to understand him and to appreciate him, and more importantly, I was now strong enough to thank him for fortifying me, for pressuring me to stick with medicine. I began to miss him, which made me realize how much I missed my friend.

BEFORE COMING HOME for the funeral. I called Gabriel. He didn't sound like I had remembered him. He was reluctant to meet with me at first, but then agreed.

"Tell me what that meeting was like," Dr. Sanders said. "It must have been very difficult for you."

I continued.

I had met him at a pool hall. We used to play a lot of pool back in the day. He had by then withdrawn from medical school. He was much heavier, but it was more than that. It was his personality. He was flat. He hardly talked or made eye contact. I don't remember much of what we talked about, but I do remember thinking, *This is not Gabriel.* He didn't say much about his decision to drop out, except that he needed time, and that eventually he wanted to give it another go. At the end of the evening I said goodbye to him. It was almost as if I was saying farewell, like he too was dead, as if I had come to town for two funerals.

"So, you were without the two people who had been most important to you?" Dr. Sanders asked.

"I think that I was moving on from them and other aspects of my life in a lot of ways. I felt less dependent, but ironically, more alone. The patriarch of my family was dead, my best friend barely recognizable, and I was searching for a place to start a practice and a new life. It was a time of seismic change for me. I had a future and a past that no longer intersected. I could do no more to please my deceased father or help my old friend."

"How about your move back to Milwaukee?" Dr. Sanders asked. "You said that you were looking to start a practice somewhere new—a fresh start. Yet you ended up back where you started."

"Well, that is true. I always had big dreams of going to some other state, to some part of the country that was new to me, or even somewhere foreign, but I never really got very far. I guess maybe I was a little homesick for my comfort zone. By this time, my girlfriend and I had married, and we were looking forward to starting a family. When we moved back to Milwaukee, I thought that it would be only for a short time. But once I started to build a practice and we began having children, it became obvious; we weren't going anywhere. It's probably part of the reason that I eventually moved to California. After all of those years in Milwaukee, I still dreamed of going places."

After twenty years of living and practicing there, I began to resent everything about Milwaukee—the crime, the racial segregation, the wintry weather. I disliked my job and even the people around me. I had mentally checked out.

"Have you traveled much Dr. Sanders?"

"Yes, some for work and a few vacations here and there. What appeals to you about traveling, Michael?"

"The beautiful thing about being somewhere different, somewhere new, is that you appreciate all of its sweetness—all of its newness. If you spend enough time there, you will also begin to appreciate those things that you have left behind, things and people and places that you had stopped seeing. In the new place there are people around you there, walking and driving, they don't see or hear or smell the things that you do. They've become unaware, almost deaf and blind to the beauty and differentness. Perhaps that's a poor analogy. If you've ever been deaf or blind, you'd know. You don't take anything for granted. That amazes me. Have you ever watched a blind person's hands, or the eyes of someone who cannot hear? Their eyes are probing, almost listening. It's the same with a blind person's hands. The loss of just one of the senses is horrible, and it is beautiful, if that makes any sense. So, if someone has all of their senses, how then is it possible for them not to miss the smell of rain or the smell of the worms on the wet sidewalk? If you have your senses, how is it possible to not see and smell the forest and the mountains and to not hear the ocean?"

"So, being somewhere different gives you back your senses."

"Yes, it's a gift, and if you don't believe that then you're not listening, and not looking. I've been given this gift, and I refuse to take it for granted, because I know that if I do it will disappear again, forever. This world we live in has beauty in every corner if you look for it. There is unimaginable horror in it, also. I know that. But I have found that in time the tragedies soften or pass, like sand blown from the surface of a rock. The beautiful things do not pass. They become even more beautiful in our minds and in our memory, as time goes by. That is a message from the universe, sent to comfort. We don't know why things happen the way they do, and we cannot. Why not then seek out the beauty? It's always been there, and it's not going anywhere."

"That's really beautiful, and true Michael. Did you just think of that now? Or is that something you have shared before with Gabriel, your father. your wife?"

"I'm not sure."

"Could they be Gabriel's words, something he shared with you, perhaps?"

"They're mine, I think."

"Just a moment ago you said, if you'd ever been deaf or blind you'd know. Why did you say that? Have you ever been deaf or blind, Michael?"

"Well I think we all have been at some time, in some way. It's a feeling of panic that you experience, I'll tell you that."

"I don't quite understand."

"It happened to me not too long ago."

"Please explain."

Everything had seemed to be going wrong for me in my job and at home. As each additional problem or malady would arise, I would figure out a way to deal with it, and smile, and carry on. I woke up one morning and I couldn't hear. Just like that! I didn't notice it at first because it was morning and there wasn't much to hear anyway. I was already awake when my phone alarm went off. I could see the phone light up, but I couldn't hear the alarm. I assumed that it was silenced, but when I picked it up, I realized that it wasn't. As I turned up the volume all of the way, I could hear it only slightly. I cursed out loud, and I could hear my voice loudly in my head, like when you put your fingers in your ears and talk.

My voice channeled through the bones of my skull, like I was underwater. I assumed that it was wax in my ears or something. I consulted with a specialist acquaintance who told me it was probably viral and would pass. Weeks went by and it didn't pass. At first, I panicked, but I dealt with it as well as I could.

"I tried to ignore the voice in my head and continue with my work, but people were beginning to notice that I seemed detached and distracted."

"How were you able to do your work if you couldn't hear and had muddled thoughts?" Dr. Sanders asked.

"It wasn't easy. I was constantly on edge, hyper-vigilant, and frustrated."

I told Dr. Sanders that during that time, a business contact reached out to me. He wanted to set up a meeting to discuss me joining the large medical group for which he served as the chief marketing officer. I was desperate to make some extra money and pay off my medical school debt. So, we met at a restaurant midday. He had no great offer for me. For me it would be more of a lateral move at best. Again, a warm body was needed, but this time it wouldn't be me.

My bothersome ear condition made it almost impossible for me to hear him in the restaurant over the sound of my own thoughts. He had a quirky personality and seemed unable to finish one sentence or one thought without getting caught up in the next. It was almost as though he was on some drug. He was very animated and never seemed to stop talking and gesticulating.

"That's how I remember it.," Dr. Sanders. "Maybe he wasn't that bad. It's likely that my lack of hearing made all of these things more exaggerated. Either way, it was an exhausting experience for me."

I had anxiously tried to read his lips. When I would talk, my voice would echo in my head so loudly that it would cause me to speak very quietly. Imagine the ridiculous scene; the two of us in a loud restaurant, this man speaking in an excited and disorganized manner, me not able to hear him, and me speaking so softly that he couldn't hear me either.

As I walked to my car after the meeting, I couldn't suppress my anger. I was starting to believe that God was fucking with me. *It must be a test. Just endure it. It's a test,* I kept thinking.

It's truly remarkable how the body and the mind can adapt and endure. It's also ironic, almost comical, or maybe even cruel, how the universe—how God works. My hands—these hands, the same ones that had been the interface between me and everything that was important to do in this life—to hold my children, to hold a hand or caress a cheek, to push aside a tear, or to paint a picture, write a letter, or in the case of a surgeon, sometimes, to save a life; these hands once lean and nimble, suddenly seemed thick and clumsy and numb. Still, I learned how to make them work.

Trying to write longhand was the worst. Writing a check took full concentration. Painting uses the arm and the hand more than the fingers, and operating—well you're wearing gloves anyway, so fine sensation is actually never there from the beginning; the brain simply learns how to interpret pressure as touch. It was much more the quiet things that had become a constant source of agitation.

"Imagine petting a dog and not being able to feel their fur. The struggling nerves begin to misinterpret and confuse the sensations; gentle touch becomes heat—heat becomes pain, Dr. Sanders. Warm water in the shower would feel like fire, yet I couldn't feel my own hair as I washed it."

"When were these sensations worse?" she asked.

"At night, when all of the other senses are quieting down, that's when my fingers came to life, vibrating, humming, throbbing, but not sleeping. At first this terrified me, then it frustrated me, then I focused on how to get by, to carry on. How can a surgeon who can't feel his fingers operate? How can an artist paint? How can a lover love? How can I sleep?"

In the end, sleeping became the most important, and the only one that I could not get around.

CHAPTER 15
The Tube

"The Tube," Ahmad Jamal, Live in Paris, 1992. A child prodigy, he began playing the piano at age three. His trios—piano, bass and drums—made groundbreaking music for sixty years. Here they are out of control, like a subway train without a driver. You can almost hear the tracks clicking by faster and faster. At some point you don't even care if the whole thing crashes, because it's just that good.

THE PREVIOUS SESSION with Dr. Sanders had drilled deep into my feelings and psyche, leaving me exhausted. The next morning, Detective Roman brought the interrogation back to the surface.

"Can we talk a little more about your training now?" he asked.

"Sure, anything in particular?"

"It sounds as though you spent a lot of time learning and training in trauma surgery while in Pittsburgh. Why was that? Were you interested in the violence?"

I just glared at him for a few seconds, trying to figure out his angle. The detective was a blunt instrument compared to Dr. Sanders.

"That's a strange way to put it, detective," I said. "No. I hated trauma before I even started my general surgery training, and I hated it even more by the time that I finished my six years of residency."

I kept my answer simple for what I perceived was a simple mind. Trauma, I told the detective, for the trauma surgeon was about the rapid systematic evaluation of the trauma patient, which then led to the best possible care and treatment for that patient. The initial evaluation in the trauma bay entailed identifying and prioritizing all of the injuries and involving all of the additional necessary specialists—orthopedics for the fractures, neurosurgery for the head injuries, urologists for any kidney or bladder injuries. Pretty much anything else was the trauma surgeon's domain. If there were any chest or abdominal injuries, the trauma surgeon would specifically take care of those. If the patient was stable, the trauma team could go about things slowly and calmly, but if they came in unstable, dying, deteriorating, circling the drain, well, then things were much more intense.

"What about burns? Was that part of the trauma surgeon's domain?"

"Not really, detective. It was its own special madness."

If a patient's only injuries were burn related, they were taken directly to a burn center. If they had other injuries, they'd initially come to a trauma center. Once those patients were stabilized regarding any other life-threatening injuries, they were shipped off to a burn center.

"I have plenty that I can tell you about burns too, if you'd like."

"Let's wait on that for now. What about trauma did you hate, Michael? It sounds fascinating and exciting."

"It does, and many people are into it. I never understood the fascination, personally. They love stories about accidents and violence—the more gruesome the better. That's why there are so many television shows about it—hospital dramas, shows about police, EMTs, and firefighters."

I didn't tell the detective this, but I had never been able to watch a single one of those for more than a few minutes before getting irritated. I couldn't tell you anything about those shows, but I could tell you a lifetime of stories about violence and blood and death—people beating each other, shooting each other, getting hit by trains, hanging themselves. The fact is, I had developed a strong aversion to violence early on. In high school I recall getting into fights and being sick afterwards if I had hurt somebody. Maybe that's part of why I wanted to be a surgeon—the helping felt better than the hurting.

As a medical student and resident, exposure to trauma was a reality—it was not optional. When I was confronted with the reality that I would have to do my shifts and rotations on the trauma service, I was very apprehensive, but I had no choice. I would make myself resistant or numb to what I was going to encounter, or at least try to. Every time that I would finish a month or two on a trauma rotation it would take a while for me to recover. Late in my training, while serving as chief resident of the trauma service, people told me that I became a different person—colder, harder. More introverted. Afterwards it would take months for me to return to baseline.

I remember one shift in particular. I was sleeping in the hospital, on duty. It was after midnight. In those days we had pagers, and more specifically, we had a type of radio pager alarm that would sound when a trauma was coming in. A dispatcher would describe the accident briefly—such as a head-on collision, high speed motor vehicle accident (MVA), gunshot wound (GSW) to the chest. You could often get an idea as to what to expect based on the description, like was the passenger ejected from the vehicle? Were there other fatalities at the scene?

We had a general term for patients in medicine and surgery that were a real mess; we called them train wrecks. On this transmission, the dispatcher said, in a very unenthusiastic voice, "We have a train wreck coming in. I mean a real train wreck—twenty-two-year-old male hit by a train." I wondered how the man was still alive. I remember thinking that, *Nobody ever survives being hit by a train.*

With that in mind, I decided that I didn't really need to rush down to the ER. I was the chief, and I didn't need to be the first one in the trauma bay. I figured, if I got there slowly enough, by the time that I arrived my junior residents and medical students would have taken care of most of the obligatory assessments on this dead trauma patient.

I slowly walked through the dimly lit late-night hospital corridors, through the peacefully empty operating rooms, and onto the trauma elevator specifically used to transport patients and personnel directly and urgently between the trauma bay and the operating rooms upstairs. The elevator would deliver me directly into the trauma bay. As the elevator passed each floor, my apprehension increased, and I tried to mentally prepare myself for the grizzly scene that awaited me once those doors opened.

Across from the elevator doors, about thirty feet away, lay the poor young man. He was on a gurney and was surrounded by students and residents. There wasn't the usual frenzy of life-saving activities because, as I had suspected, he was already dead. He must have had a pulse when they picked him up. As I approached, I didn't notice any missing limbs or a mess of blood anywhere. Some of the students and residents moved aside as I approached, but some remained on the other side of the table. Hard to imagine, but the dead young man looked very normal. As I walked around the head of the table to the other side, I noticed that half of his face and head was missing, along with his left arm and shoulder. The OMF residents (oral and maxillofacial surgeons) were bent over, hovering around the transected head, carefully pointing out the deep facial anatomy with excitement.

I had flashes of memories of Gabriel and me at the tracks. Had this guy placed his head on the rail listening for a train, to lay a coin? Or had he had enough of this life, like in Gabriel's poem? That's what I was thinking about as I walked slowly, again and again, around the table. I'm quite sure that nobody else was thinking these things. That's why I was different than them. That's why I always have been. They were amazed and invigorated; I couldn't sleep afterwards.

I never returned to those train tracks after that last time with Gabriel, but after I moved back to Milwaukee, sometimes I would drive by that field, near the home where I had grown up. I could see the spot in the distance where we used to sit under the freeway. In my mind I would always see that young man's face.

CHAPTER 16
Dig Dis

Hank Mobley—the middleweight champion of the tenor sax comes full speed with this 1960 recording on the Blue Note label "Dig Dis." 6:09. Wynton Kelly's piano struts out first, and the bass of Paul Chambers nods in agreement. Art Blakey's drumroll is like an avalanche of gravel, and Hank comes running around the corner to join the strut. Swingin' straight ahead hard bop classic from the champ.

I WAS BEGINNING to feel a little stronger, but I would get anxious when I'd think about the eventuality of leaving the hospital and going back to work. I wasn't healed yet. If anything, I was beginning to feel worse. I started to think about my current job, and the ugly side of my livelihood.

I remembered standing silently, listening to the proctor at the liposuction clinic repeat the familiar message to a patient—part sales pitch, and part truth. The proctor's job is to train and direct surgeons in the clinic, and in my case, his instruction was often an insult. After all, I had been a surgeon for twenty-five years, and although I didn't know liposuction, I had more years of surgical training and surgical experience than him. That bred in me, and I suspect others in our practice, a bitterness. Even so, I had to acknowledge that the man was in his position for a reason, and he had things to teach me. If I was going to make big money, I would have to pay close attention to him, regardless of how humiliating it was. I remembered his voice clearly, as if standing beside him.

"This is fat we can remove. Here is an area of asymmetry that we will try to improve, but we will not be able to achieve perfection. The scars are permanent and will never completely disappear, but we will try to hide them. These are folds or flexure points. They may become more noticeable once fat is removed. I strongly recommend that you purchase the pubic area as well or it may look a little funny once the abdomen is flatter."

Some of these details were given to assure that the patient received the best advice. Some of the details were to develop appropriate expectations. Along with pre-operative photos, all these details were documented, to have a record, when and if there was dissatisfaction.

The embarrassed patient stood in front of the full-length mirror in a tiny company-issued bikini that allowed no confinement of their fat. The imperfections were displayed for all in the crowded room as the patient turned from front view to side view, always keeping an eye on their image in the mirror, imagining a new body without this bulge or that roll. There were some who had previously undergone cosmetic surgery of some sort. These patients were more confident, almost enthusiastically ready for the next round. I watched the proctor use his purple marking pen to draw the lines identifying the anatomic landmarks and accentuating the areas to be suctioned. I would soon be drawing on the patients and pitching this same plan, with some personal variations, once given the green light by the proctor.

Some patients came to us in pursuit of a transformation, others hoping for a specific improvement. Some wanted to look perfect, but most, like the one we were about to lipo, just wanted to look better in clothes. Although the results were often somewhat unnatural, they were dramatic. The before and after pictures showed obvious improvements.

Sometimes the after photo was almost unrecognizable—so improved from the before body.

Once the interview and drawings were complete and the consent was signed, the patient was given oral pain and anti-anxiety medication to help them better tolerate the awake procedure. *Before* photos were taken of the front, left side, right side, and back views. The proctor and I would leave the room. At the station in the hallway we would determine how many bags of numbing solution would be required to accomplish the plan. These one-liter bags of IV fluids containing a precise amount of numbing and vasoconstriction medications would later be instilled under the skin and into the fat layer of the areas to be suctioned. My job was to retreat to a small closet-like room where I would inject the bags with the proper amounts of these medications. This was typically the best part of the day, usually about five minutes during which I was alone. My every movement was not being observed. I wasn't in anybody's way. The small room was warm due to the steam sterilizing autoclave. I liked that. It was essential to put the precise amount of medications in each bag, based on the weight of the patient and the number of areas being addressed. A mistake could have possibly life-threatening complications. Still, I felt comfortable with this task. After all, I had been a surgeon for so many years. I was used to taking every detail seriously, every day.

The proctor had been strict in his instructions. He treated everybody in the clinic as though they were children, especially me. There was only one way to lay out the bags onto the table. There was a specific choreographed way in which to set out the bottles of medications. There was only one proper technique to tear open an alcohol wipe and swipe the rubber tops of each bottle and the injection sites on the IV bags. Most specific was the way I was instructed to use the syringes to draw up the meds, and finally to label each bag with a huge sticker specifying its contents. It was almost like teaching a chef the only proper way to butter a piece of bread, even though he had been buttering bread for over a quarter of a century. As I lay in the hospital bed reliving this, I had to admit that the proctor's routine was efficient and minimized the potential for errors.

I had stacked the IV bags on top of each other in the precise bowling pin arrangement that I had been taught, and then I carried the six bags into the operating room.

CHAPTER 17
Stolen Moments

"Stolen Moments," 8:45 from Oliver Nelson's 1961 landmark release *The Blues and The Abstract Truth*, On the Impulse label. Oliver's tenor and Eric Dolphy's alto sing together, but it's Freddie Hubbard's trumpet that is like a splash of cold water in your face. The saxophones and flute dance with him then to the end beautifully.

DR. SANDERS WANTED some alone time with me, out of earshot of Detective Roman and his interruptions. The two, it seemed, were on divergent paths. She wanted to explore more deeply what my life was like after residency in Pittsburgh, after I moved back to Milwaukee, and why I reconnected with Gabriel.

"Why all of the curiosity about Gabriel?" I asked.

"Michael, understanding that relationship, its significance, may provide some insights into your personnel struggles, things that you may not be fully aware of, things that are beneath the surface."

"Dr. Sanders, I'm still not even sure why I am in here and under your care. I'm the victim here, the guy who was shot. Remember?"

"Michael, there are things that have occurred that you may not be aware of or remember. I am here to help you sort those out. I promise, you'll have more clarity if you just stick with this."

"Okay Doc. I'll hang in there, but at some point, I need to know where this is heading."

"Deal, Michael."

And so I began again, conjuring thoughts and memories of my dearest friend.

Garbriel had seemed transformed and almost unrecognizable when I had met him in the pool hall when I came home for my father's funeral. This time, he had somehow, as if by some dark magic, once again become the friend that I had known all of those years. I wondered whether he had made a deal with God or the devil? He told me that he had found a good doctor and that he was on better meds now.

"I know it's hard to believe Dr. Sanders, but it was like we had never missed a beat. All of those years of my training in surgery and him in and out of psychiatric facilities, and here we were talking and laughing like nothing had changed. I guess it was foolish of me and naive to think that we could carry on like always—pick up where we had left off—but at the time I was just so happy to have him back. Who could blame me for believing in miracles?"

Gabriel was trying to get back on track and put his life back together. He did odd jobs, even substitute teaching, while he plotted his return to medical school. I didn't really think that it was possible for someone with mental illness to become a physician, but doctors are people too.

Gabriel would spend a lot of time in the downtown public library. He was supposed to be studying to retake the medical school entrance exam, but I think that deep down he knew that he would never gain admission into another medical school. He confided that he was actually kicked out for dangerous behavior and poor academic performance—not that he had voluntarily dropped out or taken a leave of absence.

Similar to me in the college campus bookstore a decade earlier, there were a lot of distractions at the library for a mind like Gabriel's.

I imagine that he spent hours browsing the aisles and bookshelves and very little time reviewing biology. The library also had a voluminous collection of jazz CDs that Gabriel would bring home for the two of us to burn into our collections. We slipped back into our old routines, listening to obscure jazz that he had found in the library, and talking about the future—our plans. The difference was that now I had crossed over. I was no longer a struggling outcast. I had accomplished what I had set out to do—at least the first stage. I had a wife. He had none of those things. He was moving backward, falling farther from his dream.

I tried to be supportive of his efforts to resume medical training, but I knew it would never happen. More than that, I had lived through that hell, and I knew that he would never survive the punishing hours and abuse of residency. It was the rigors of medical school that had caused him to snap in the first place. He would never survive the challenges that came after graduation.

I avoided mentioning Gabriel's failing, hoping to push that chapter into the background. Instead, I supported his renewed enthusiasm for treating patients and medical science by encouraging his pursuit of a degree in nursing. Gabriel embraced the idea and rebooted his life and career. He would have to take a few supplemental college courses, but after med school we thought those would be a breeze.

Gabriel slowly re-emerged as he once had been—more like family than a friend to me, like a brother who was down on his luck but bouncing back. I brought him into our house for the holidays and paid for every drink and every meal we had out. Still, at the end of the night, I would drop him off at his government-subsidized apartment, at his psychiatric stalemate of a life, and return to my wife and my children and my career. I wondered all along how healthy this really was for him to straddle my world and his, but he never did seem resentful. To me the alternative of him being alone always seemed worse.

He told me secrets, at least that's what I thought of them; these were details of his descent into psychosis. After he had been kicked out of medical school for erratic and violent behavior, he felt that he needed to go to Peru to visit his extended family. Once there, his behavior became even more bizarre. Eventually, he began living in the streets and sleeping in cemeteries. He told me that he felt at home among the graves. At night, his ancestors would admonish him in Spanish, further agitating him. He was eventually arrested when wandering the streets of Lima. It was then that he was first hospitalized.

Through the combined efforts of his mother and her relatives in Peru, he was transported back to the US and continued treatment here. He was heavily medicated during that period and did not really remember much detail. The initial treatment for schizophrenia or bipolar disease was quite aggressive. Heavy doses of medications were administered to bring him out of that psychotic state. He had existed in a trance-like condition while the medications were slowly tapered to a more functional dose, or the determined optimal combination of medications was decided upon.

"Yesterday you told the detective and me that one of the reasons that you decided to leave Milwaukee and move to California was because things *went bad* with Gabriel. What did you mean by that?" Dr. Sanders asked.

"Gabriel was on a much better drug regimen than when I first reconnected with him. Still, he was never happy with the side effects," I explained. "They affected his energy and motivation and creativity. That's why he would sometimes stop taking his meds, and that's exactly what happened."

ONE DAY I received a call from his mother. She told me that he was not returning any of her phone calls. I could hear the concern in her voice as she asked me if I could help. I tried calling Gabriel myself for several days, but without success. So, I went to his place to check on him. By then, he had moved into a small apartment above a garage in a dicey neighborhood on Milwaukee's south side. I walked down the long driveway and up the stairway that ran along the side of the garage up to the space. At the top of the steps was a door with a window. I peered inside but didn't see him. I knocked but there was no reply. The door was unlocked, so I entered slowly so as not to frighten him.

The air was still and warm. It was completely silent except for the sound of some flies buzzing around an uneaten pork chop on the kitchen table. The place was in disarray. Mostly there were dishes everywhere, and clothes. I saw Gabriel over on a cot against the wall. He was sitting, leaning back against the wall. He didn't look at me. I went over to speak with him. I told him how much we were worried about him, and that I was there to help. I'd told him that I would help him clean up, and that it wasn't healthy to live like this. I asked him about his meds. The whole time he didn't speak or move, or change his expression, or even look at me. After about twenty minutes I gave up and left.

Reluctantly, I told his mother the details—how I had failed to get anywhere with Gabriel. I felt he was almost catatonic. She said that she would talk to his doctors and see what they could do.

I don't know how they eventually managed to get him out of that apartment, but weeks later, I went to visit him in the psychiatric facility. He was quiet and sad, almost embarrassed. He seemed like someone who had planned an escape from prison, only to be captured and brought back to his cell. I looked around the place. It was almost like a movie scene. Everyone was sedated and most were sitting alone quietly. There were tables with puzzles and board games that nobody was playing. There was a television on that nobody was watching. I seemed to be the only visitor.

"We looked each other in the eyes. We were faced with the reality that there would be no escape."

CHAPTER 18
Diamonds On My Windshield

Tom Waits, "Diamonds on My Windshield" off the 1974 album The Heart of Saturday Night. It's a late-night freeway ride complete with the gravel of Waits' voice and the frenetic bass of Jim Hughart. After speeding through the late-night sights, it's one more block, the engine talks, and whispers home at last.

DR. SANDERS TOOK some notes and remained silent for a few moments, obviously digesting what she had just heard. I sat in my hospital bed shoulders slumped and feeling drained.

"Are you okay?" she asked. "Would you like to keep going? I feel like we're making progress on exploring the significance of your relationship with Gabriel."

I took a deep breath and a sip of water and nodded. "Unburdening myself is stressful, but maybe it's helping. Yes, let's keep going."

"Let's back up a bit, Michael. Tell me about how you dealt with Gabriel during those years when you rekindled your relationship with him in Milwaukee."

"I could relate to Gabriel's despair," I started. "He felt trapped, like there was no way out. That's when an animal, or a person is most dangerous."

"Not very much different than the situation you later found yourself in just a few months ago. Am I right?"

"I guess you have a point there." I chuckled.

"You both had been through traumatic experiences and struggled to escape the life you were born into. You both found yourselves fighting against forces that ultimately were out of your control. I think that may be the root of your bond. You're not that different, the two of you. You see so much of yourself in him."

"I didn't realize it then, but I am beginning to see that now, Dr. Sanders."

"Please continue, Michael. Tell me some more about what happened next."

WHEN GABRIEL WAS released from the psychiatric hospital, I picked him up and we just drove. I didn't tell him where we were going for a long while. I turned onto the freeway, and we headed to Chicago. During my surgical internship in Chicago I had discovered the landmark jazz club—The Green Mill, which I had referenced earlier. Back in the 1920's it was mob-owned, and Al Capone's favorite hangout. His favorite booth was still there, along with a trap door hatch to an underground escape tunnel. As I mentioned, Gabriel and I both loved jazz. We had some great nights at The Green Mill, digging the live music and the history of the place. I was hoping that this drive would give us some time to talk and figure things out. For a while, as we drove, he just stared up through the windshield at the expressway lights passing over us. As we drove out of the Milwaukee suburbs and into the farmland the lies between Milwaukee and Chicago, the freeway lights disappeared, and he finally said something.

"The raindrops are like little diamonds on your windshield. Like that Tom Waits song."

"What's going on in your head Gabriel?" I asked.

"I'm afraid of myself. Can you imagine that? How can you live when you are afraid of yourself? I know that what's going on is not under my control, and that scares me. Everyone has to deal with the fact that they can't control the world around them, but I have to accept that I cannot control my own thoughts and actions. It's this disease."

There was a long silence. I searched for some way to pretend that I could even vaguely relate to what he was going through.

"You're right. I guess maybe try to think of it more like any other medical condition, like diabetes. If you have diabetes you can't control your blood sugars without medication. You don't have to be ashamed of that. Just don't stop taking you meds again."

"Yeah, it sounds simple, but it's not really. When I get tired of the meds, I stop for a while. Then I can really feel the difference. It feels good at first and I am confident that it's the right move. I feel energized—alive. The longer that I'm off them though, everything starts to change, and it all gets worse. I lose control and all judgment, but at the time I am unaware of that. It escalates like that for weeks. I don't sleep for days, then I black out. Next thing I know, I'm in some hospital somewhere. Man, you can't imagine what it was like the first time being in a psychiatric ward, surrounded by crazy people. That's what I am. Can you believe that?"

He continued.

"When I'm back on the meds most things are better, but some are not. I feel my brain gel, like it's in wet cement. My emotions get slow and blunted. My creativity gets caged up then. When I'm on those pills I don't even want to look in the mirror. I'm afraid of myself. And I don't want to look around at other people. Hell, I don't even look up at the sky. Sometimes I do it without thinking—look up at the evening sky. When I realize what I am doing, I look away, almost like I'm ashamed. Why should that happen to me? I'm not sure why the stars affect me so, but they do. I guess that maybe the vastness is so overwhelming that it brings disturbing thoughts into my mind. Other people, they seek out the stars, gaze at them for hours, study them, write poems about them, even travel in them. I fear them man. I don't want to know what they know because it makes everything that I know seem ridiculous and irrelevant."

That was such a sad notion, to be afraid to look at the sky, as though it was mocking you, and judging you, yet having to live under that sky, always. I pushed those words and those thoughts out of my brain and tried to cheer Gabriel up a little. "We're going to The Mill baby, The Green Mill! You know not even those fucking pills can keep you from digging that place. I don't know who's playing, but I'm sure it will be hot."

He smiled and seemed to loosen up a bit. When we got there, we stood for a while, then we found a spot at the bar. The night had turned cold. Outside, it had started to snow. Inside, it was warm and humid as we squinted in the dim light for an open spot at the long L-shaped bar. The doorway led into the long portion of the L, a skinny walkway along the bar, then opened into the small main room with a central stage and a grand piano. We found a perfect spot at the elbow of the bar. I ordered drinks and sat there quietly, looking around. I had always loved places like The Mill, places trapped in time. I love to watch the people—the couples at the little tables with the vintage candles, the people talking close, touching each other. They talk loudly but respectfully, adding a background buzz to the musical performance. I remember sitting there and wishing that I could play the sax like that guy up on stage. I think that I could have been very happy sitting on a little stool, putting it all out there night after night, making just enough to pay for my rent and my food and cigarettes. I think that I would have slept well every night, because I would have been up there yelling to the universe, talking to God. Who wouldn't want to be able to talk to God every fucking night?

Each time that I looked over at Gabriel, I noticed that he wasn't watching the band, or listening to the music. He was staring the other way, down the long bar, out the windows at the falling snow. People were walking by the glass door and windows, struggling in the snow, going somewhere. They were moving. The band was playing. Snow was falling. I'd like to say that I knew what he was thinking that night, but I didn't have a clue what was going on inside his head. He turned to me and offered a cigarette. He loved to smoke American Spirit cigarettes. He thought that because they were preservative-free they were healthier. The pack had a picture of an Indian chief in profile. Gabriel, being from Peru, I think he felt close to the native spirits, their history and culture. We smoked a couple, watched the scene, and listened to the band. I put my hand on his shoulder and looked him in the eyes. We both smiled, and I ordered a couple more drinks. I'd like to say that we had a great evening, but it was just okay. We both had a lot on our minds. I think that the drinks helped. I had introduced him to the highball.

He slept on the drive back. I remember thinking that this has got to work. I thought that he would be more careful from now on, and that, really, anything was possible for him. I thought that wanting it to be so would make it so, but that's not how it works. He would never fulfill his dream to be a medical doctor. We both knew that. His world was getting small, and his horizon was being reigned in.

He spent that night at my house and the next day I took him back to his studio above the garage. We cleaned it up together. He seemed to be in a better mood. While we were there the landlord knocked on the door. Gabriel went out onto the steps to talk with him for a few minutes. The conversation was too quiet for me to hear. When he returned, he had a distant look on his face. We kept cleaning. I waited for him to tell me what was said, but he didn't. I could pretty much figure out what the conversation was about, but I was hopeful that maybe this time I was wrong. Maybe the old guy came to welcome Gabriel back and offer him some encouraging words.

"Nope. He told me I have to leave," Gabriel confided. "Said I was unstable and scary. Gave me one month to get out."

CHAPTER 19
Lush Life

It's Coltrane again. For me, to really appreciate this tune, I had to first hear the 1963 version of John Coltrane with singer Johnny Hartman, "Lush Life" 5:29. The words are the key, so beautiful and true. The tune builds toward optimism, then falls back down to Earth. Every day is back to the same, and it settles into acceptance—so important. When Coltrane finally comes in, it's sweet, with layers of all the hopes and dreams, some of them still in play. Go back then to the 1961 Coltrane album's title track, "Lush Life", 13:55. It's Paul Chambers on bass, Red Garland piano, Donald Byrd trumpet. This version is more distilled for me. It speaks without words. Red speaks the same words as Coltrane, but in a different language. It's almost ten minutes before Byrd's trumpet comes in to emphasize. Then he's there till the end. The tune sums it all up and is a commentary that demands attention.

I WASN'T AS emotionally or physically strong as I thought. Baring my soul to Dr. Sanders about Gabriel sapped my energy, and the next day I didn't feel well. I asked the doctor if we could cancel our session. There was something strange going on, as if I was emerging from a fog. I was starting to get agitated. I had a subtle uneasy feeling. Things weren't adding up. The detective was grilling me like a criminal. I didn't trust him. I was a victim.

I knew that I had suffered a vicious attack and had almost died from the hemorrhage. I had undergone extensive abdominal surgery and had been unconscious in the ICU for six weeks. I am a surgeon for Christ's sake; I knew what had happened to me, but I didn't know who did it.

The following day I confronted Dr. Sanders with my frustration. I told her that I didn't get it. I felt as if I was being interrogated, especially by the detective, but also by her as if I was under suspicion for attacking myself.

"I mean shouldn't he be out looking for the person who almost killed me? Why is he wasting his time here when he should be out there finding the shooter?"

"Detective Roman is, Michael. I am, well, we are both just trying to get as much information as we can about you and Gabriel, because some things just aren't adding up. Do you see that? We're just trying to fill in the blanks. Does that make sense?"

"I'm not sure," I said, exasperated.

"Well let's keep going then. There may be some details that will help all of us. Our last conversation ended with Gabriel's eviction, right? What was going on after that?"

AT THIS TIME Gabriel was really struggling. What made it more difficult is that I had entered into a prosperous and productive period in my life. I was building my surgery practice and living in a beautiful home, with a beautiful family. Gabriel had become a fixture in our life. He continued to pursue nursing school, taking a few classes here and there, but he seemed unable to focus. Whenever the level of stress built up to a certain point, he would bail. He had developed an unsettling routine. He would work different jobs, but couldn't make too much money, or he would lose his disability assistance with his rent and food stamps and health insurance. He had become comfortable with that existence, and I had accepted it, too.

"To be honest, Dr. Sanders, I felt at the time like I was taking advantage of him instead of the other way around."

She had a confused look on her face. "How could that be? You were always very good to him. I don't see how you could feel that you were taking advantage of him."

"Yeah, that's true, but you must understand that I was also benefiting from this arrangement. Basically, he was always an enthusiastic participant in whatever it was that I wanted to do, and he was always available. Want to watch a football game... call Gabriel. Want to go to a concert or jazz club... call Gabriel. All that I had to do was pay for everything. It annoyed my wife sometimes, but it served Gabriel and me well.

"Okay, so you were friends who did things together. Why feel guilty about that, Michael?"

"He was there for me, but I wasn't always there for him in the same way, in his quiet and lonely moments. I lived my life and wasn't available every time that Gabriel needed me—only when it was convenient for me. You see what I mean?"

At the time, I was also not sure that the constant exposure to the good life, the type of life he had always wanted and would never have, wasn't harmful to his psyche, in a way emphasizing his failures, I explained.

"I convinced myself that I was being a good friend, and doing what was best for him. As it turned out, I really wasn't, but it continued that way for years."

Dr. Sanders steered the conversation in a different direction.

"Those were good years for you. You were a burn surgeon, isn't that right?" she asked.

"I was. I never wanted to be a burn surgeon, but I just happened to be in the wrong place at the wrong time I guess."

"I would imagine that it was very difficult. If you didn't want to be a burn surgeon, why and how did you end up doing it for all of those years?' she asked.

"It's ironic," I said. "Who would have guessed that the little kid in the hospital who was terrified by the burned child in the bed next to him would go on to become a burn surgeon?"

I had experience in burns during my training. When I began practice in Milwaukee I was approached by the head of the department. They needed another burn surgeon. I needed the money. I thought it would be temporary. As it turned out, I was very good at it, and that made it very difficult to turn my back on those patients, even if I didn't want to do it anymore.

"The years passed, and eventually I couldn't find a way out. In the end, it was one of the reasons that I moved to California."

"What specifically did you dislike about it?" the doctor asked.

"It's a tough specialty. It's gruesome. It's heartbreaking. It wore me out."

I explained that most burns are not the result of some freak accident. There are the occasional unavoidable events like being struck by lightning. But the majority of accidents that result in significant burns and end up in a burn center result from stupidity, drugs and alcohol, and violence. Someone is cleaning something with gasoline and stops to have a cigarette; someone tries to burn wet leaves or garbage by pouring gasoline on it; some kid throws an aerosol can into a bonfire causing it to explode sending hot embers into the faces of a group of teenage cheerleaders; a jealous girlfriend throws hot bacon grease onto her cheating boyfriend; a couple cooking meth in a trailer and there is a chemical explosion; a drunk grandmother falls out of her wheelchair into the campfire.

"House fires were often the worst. If the person doesn't die of the severe burns, then they would often succumb to the smoke inhalation."

There was one group of burn patients that had disturbed me most—the mentally ill, usually those who are schizophrenic.

"These are the only patients I ever encountered who try to commit suicide by setting themselves on fire. Voices tell them to do it. And if they survive after months in the hospital, they go out and try to do it again. Only the schizophrenics did that."

"Yes, I am aware of that behavior," Dr. Sanders said. "Self-destructive behavior can be horrifying on several levels."

I briefly described the bloody and gruesome surgeries required to remove the burned skin and fat and replace it with thin layers of unburned skin from other areas of the body. The patient's own donor skin is run through a meshing device so that it can be stretched to cover the largest possible area. The site is bandaged for a week as the skin slowly grows like grass seed. The patients have one or two surgeries every week, and when the thin donor site skin regrows, you go back and use it again. You keep on doing that over and over until everything is covered with new skin. As you can imagine, the healed burns don't look anything like normal skin. The patients are in the hospital for months. Many die from infection or other complications.

Some of the worse burn victims were placed on a ventilator and sedated for months. I had often feared that when they would finally awaken and see their scars and contracted joints, their contorted faces, I was sure that they would ask me why I hadn't just let them die.

"You know what the amazing part is, Dr. Sanders? They never did—not once. They had this unexplainable resilience and gratitude for being alive. It was almost as if they came out of those flames with all of the disfigurement, but also with a wonderful gift. That did inspire me."

I was lost in my thoughts for a while, looking down at my slippers when finally, her voice brought me back.

"I can understand why you felt that you needed to stop. You shouldn't be ashamed or have any guilt for your decision to move on from that part of your career, Michael."

"I did that job for twenty years, and it took its toll. I couldn't separate myself emotionally from my patients. The empathy and pity

I felt for these poor people started affecting my judgment. The clinical side of me felt at odds with my emotional being."

"You haven't talked much about that before. I knew that you had felt conflicted about being a doctor, but this provides more clarity. It makes more sense now."

"I've tried to put it behind me. You know, I've known surgeons who could go to sleep at night no matter what had happened at work. They would witness the most horrible of scenarios and it wouldn't affect them. People would sometimes die. That was part of this business we simply accepted. They seemed always able to figure out how to explain it all away and start the next day unfazed. I could never do that. Everything stuck with me. I couldn't save everyone. I couldn't look in the mirror. I couldn't sleep."

CHAPTER 20
Here I Am

Donald Byrd, on Blue Note, the 1959 Hard Bop album Byrd in Hand. "Here I Am," 8:25. The man is working with his sextet. The sound of the trumpet and two saxophones is a rare ingredient that you don't get to taste often. Charlie Rouse on tenor, Pepper Adams baritone, Walter Davis Jr. piano, Sam Jones bass and Art Taylor drums. The baritone and the tenor are a beautiful swinging contrast to Byrd's sharp and melodic trumpet. Charlie sits down with a cup of coffee; Pepper can't keep his cool. Walter and the rhythm section hold it all together, like "Hey man, let's talk it over. I'm ready for whatever you have to say to me. Here I am.

DAYS PRIOR, DETECTIVE Roman had asked me to cut out the unnecessary details, to be more concise. Apparently, he had little patience—and perhaps a short attention span. I had news for him. If he wanted me to empty out my head to him, he was going to indulge me from time to time. The jazz stuff relaxes me, takes me to a different place. Dr. Sanders had come to my rescue on that.

"You should know that we've been recording your sessions with Dr. Sanders, and I've reviewed the last couple of days. Correct me if

I'm wrong, but it sounds like you and Gabriel were pretty simpatico. What happened? When did things start to go south?"

"I have already covered that ground with Dr. Sanders. And shouldn't she be here too?" I asked.

"Sure Doc, if that makes you more comfortable."

"Michael please—and yes, I'd prefer that."

When Dr. Sanders joined us, she had a cup of coffee for me, real coffee, not decaf. Initially I wouldn't drink anything that they offered me, out of concern that maybe one of them had put something in it, like a drug to sedate me or make me less guarded or more revealing. It smelled so good. Up to this point, I hadn't been allowed to drink regular coffee because the caffeine interacted with my meds.

Detective Roman and Dr. Sanders spoke privately for a few minutes as if negotiating a compromise. When they returned, the detective asked about when things had started to turn sour between Gabriel and me while in Milwaukee.

"Did he start behaving badly when he went off his meds? Is that when you cut him off?

"He did fall off the wagon, so to speak—a self-imposed medication holiday," I said. "It ended him right back in the usual spot. He would stabilize, make some progress in school or on a job, but then backslide. Honestly detective, it was hard to watch and be around."

"Go on, Michael," Dr. Sanders encouraged.

"I was frustrated that Gabriel couldn't sustain momentum with anything he attempted. He would have a few good weeks at some new job, or take classes to become a nurse, or whatever. But he always regressed. He always would end up back at square one. It was heartbreaking to watch because he is a smart guy. I think that he could have been successful, and independent, and happy. I kept wanting that for him—wanting him to pull himself out of this cycle—but maybe that was not fair or realistic."

"He was mentally ill, on meds. You knew that. You're a doctor," Detective Roma blurted. "Did you really think this guy could have a normal life?"

"I guess I was in denial, detective. Gabriel was a sick man living on public assistance who would never get better. He couldn't handle the unavoidable stress that's comes with living an independent life. I think he realized that too, or maybe it was a crutch. Either way, he chose to stay on public assistance. I think he saw it as his only option, so he settled into that routine. I was wrong for expecting anything more of him."

"You said that Gabriel would often have relapses. What was that like, Michael," Dr. Sanders asked.

"There was a similarity to all of them, but let me tell you about one in particular."

WHEN GABRIEL WAS living downtown in his subsidized apartment, he had made some friends. They were not the best influence on him. They were mostly unemployed and aimless, spending much of the day on the couch playing video games and smoking pot. In the evenings they would go out to clubs and try to meet women. That's how Gabriel met his girlfriend. She was from the neighborhood, and they started dating, if you want to call it that. It had progressed to the point where he was actually spending most nights at her place.

I had met her. Although she had her quirks, I liked her. She seemed responsible and independent. I was glad that he had found someone other than me that he could be close to. His relationship with her took a lot of pressure off me, and I was grateful. I had wondered if she knew about his illness, or, if he relapsed, how long it would be before she decided that she'd had enough. My answer came sooner than I had expected.

Gabriel had called me one day as I was pulling into work. He seemed normal at first. Then he began telling me that his girlfriend was cheating on him. She was having sex with his friends, in his apartment when he wasn't there. For a few moments I was like, *Holy crap, are you kidding me?* Then I realized that he was having paranoid delusions. He had never caught his girlfriend with anyone, he had only imagined it. I questioned him about whether he had stopped taking his meds. He didn't want to talk about that. He avoided the question and kept on with his suspicions. I tried to calm him down, but everything I said was met with an argument. I remember thinking that I was grateful that, even in this state, he still felt that he could trust me. I told him that I had to go to work but that I would call him later and we could talk more about it. I asked him not to confront anybody until we had a chance to talk. It bugged me all that day. I remember that. I had trouble focusing on my work.

Later that night I had called him, but he didn't answer. I left a message. Have you ever had something bad happen, like really bad, and you think maybe it didn't really happen, and if you don't think about it maybe it will go away, but it doesn't go away? That's what this felt like for me. I hoped that maybe he'd realized the mistake he had made and would start taking his meds again. Maybe the next time I talked to him perhaps he'd be back to normal. I called him a few times to no avail. I hoped that he'd call me back eventually, but he didn't, so I let some time pass. On the third day I called again and left another message.

The next day, after work, I went to his apartment building and rang his buzzer. He didn't say anything, but I heard the intercom come on. I told him who I was through the speaker. Again, he didn't say anything, but he buzzed me in. I went down the hallway to his door and knocked on it. There was no answer. The door was locked. I put my ear up against it and listened. I could hear him shuffling around, but he wouldn't answer me or let me in. I told him that I wanted to talk about what was going on, that I was worried about him and that I wanted to help him if I could. Once again, he didn't answer.

The next day I went back. It was dark and raining. This time he didn't answer the doorbell, he didn't buzz me in. His apartment was on the ground level, so I crept around through the wet bushes, to his window to see if I could see him. I figured that he was maybe in that catatonic state again. It was dark inside. The sheer drapes were closed, and I couldn't see or hear anything. I went back to my car and sat there in the rain for a while, thinking that maybe I'd see him come or go, but no luck.

That night I contacted his mother and told her what was going on. She told me that she was aware. She said that his sisters had stopped allowing him to come over to visit and to see their children because he seemed disoriented and agitated. They were afraid of him.

I went to the police station in his neighborhood. I explained his medical condition and his behavior. I told them that I was concerned about him and what he might do. Again, I was being naive. There are rules and laws regarding these sorts of things, which you only learn about if you are unfortunate enough to have to. They told me that they couldn't do anything unless there was credible proof that he posed a risk of harm to himself or to others. I knew that he did pose that risk, but that was not enough for them. They needed him to actually hurt himself or someone else before they could step in. It's a protection created to prevent unnecessary and involuntary hospitalization, but in doing so it allowed very sick people to languish with their illness, until disaster occurs. I don't know what the solution is but there must be some middle ground between the two extremes.

Days went by and I became more and more desperate. For all I knew, he could be lying dead in his apartment. I couldn't find anyone who would help me. A friend told me about a website where you could enter someone's name, and it would pull up any arrests or legal actions against that person. I wanted to know if perhaps he was already in custody or hospitalized. I went to the site, and I was shocked to see a photo of Gabriel's angry face. The text below described a recent misdemeanor arrest for damaging property. Apparently, he had used a bat to damage the vehicle of someone who had taken his parking spot. He had recently been in a minor car accident and didn't even have a car to park in that spot. Apparently, that had been enough to push him over the edge. I figured that this must be credible evidence. Once again, I contacted the police, who told me that damage to property does not constitute a risk of harm to self or others. Again, I had hit a dead end.

Soon after that, a strange game of cat and mouse ensued. It was almost as if he was aware of my efforts with the police. He began calling me. He began toying with me. He'd try to bait me—draw me into an argument, but I wouldn't fall for that. I remained clinical, and caring—never letting him anger me or frustrate me, or at least not letting him see that. Even though I knew that he was mentally ill and delusional, and even to the point of psychosis, up to this point the things that he said always had just enough truth in them to give me pause, if even just for a moment. It seemed different this time—angry, violent.

He had never seen me as a threat before. Now, I too had become his enemy. Finally, he began accusing me, and I had become the sharpened focus of his paranoia. I too was sleeping with his girl, in his bed. I was the ultimate Judas. He could focus his disorganized hallucinations now on me. It didn't matter what I said or tried; I couldn't sway him. The phone calls usually ended with him hanging up on me, or with me hanging up—just to end it, and to regroup.

I knew a detective at the police department; we weren't friends really, but our kids were in the same elementary school and played sports together. I reached out to him. He looked into it and had a few of his guys go to Gabriel's place to convince him that he should stop harassing people, me in particular. That wasn't really my intention. I wanted them to get him to someplace safe where he could get some help. Of course, this was doomed to fail. I imagine that whatever interaction that they had with him, they likely tried to intimidate or threaten him. In Gabriel's irrational state, these actions only seemed to fuel the fire.

What happened next was chilling. I was shaving in the morning, and he called my cell. I put down the razor and sat down to talk to him. The conversation took its usual bizarre course with exaggerated and inappropriate responses. There were long silent pauses, but I had decided not to react, but to just be patient and see if somehow, I could reach him. Finally, he broke the silence. He told me that he needed me to come over and clean up his apartment, that he had made a really bad mess, and after I was done, he was going to chop me up in his meat grinder just like her. I was in shock. My closest friend had become unrecognizable, a dangerous predator. I was concerned that he had hurt his girlfriend. I was afraid for my safety. How could this have happened so quickly?

I had been trying to help him for as long as I could remember, and now I was beginning to think that all I really did was harm him. Images of what he could have done in his apartment flashed through my mind and I froze there. I muttered something like, "I can't come over there. I have to take my kids to school."

"I know where your kids go to school. Maybe I'll stop by there later."

CHAPTER 21
Judgement

Andrew Hill, "Judgement" 6:54, recorded in 1964. The Chicago-born pianist seems to emerge from the shadow of Thelonius Monk. The Blue Note album cover shows him leaning up against a brick wall just outside a tunnel of darkness. The tune is upbeat and optimistic with the vibes of Billy Hutcherson, but Elvin Jones sneaks in a drum solo that says, "Don't delude yourself man, this isn't going to end well."

THE DETECTIVE'S SMUGNESS, what little of it there had been, quickly dissipated when hearing of Gabriel's threat to my children.

"Is that south enough for you detective?" I asked.

"Well, we're getting there." he said somberly. "Please continue, Michael. How did you respond to the threat?"

"I was freaked. I dropped the phone and sat there for a while with my face half shaven. My first thoughts were those of panic and rage. I was concerned for my children. I was also furious that Gabriel would turn on me like this. I took some deep breaths, and then I stood up and finished shaving. I reminded myself that he was sick."

I had looked into that mirror, into my eyes, at exactly who I had become. I felt as though I had in some way created this mess; maybe we all had a part in it, our jacked-up society so focused on success, one that I was now very much a part of. Maybe we all are somewhat responsible, I told the detective.

What am I going to do now, I thought. I refused to let Gabriel's psychosis shake me. In defiance, I took my kids to school, and I went to work, as if there was nothing wrong. But there was something terribly wrong. My mind raced all morning and, finally overwhelmed, I collapsed during surgery. The nurses and operating room techs sat me down and gave me some water. I didn't tell them everything, but I did tell them that someone close to me had been threatening my family. I couldn't hold it together, and I began to cry. It took some time for me to calm down again. I assured everyone that I was alright, then I scrubbed my hands again to complete the surgery. I could see them all watching me closely as I worked, wondering what was really going on.

Before work I had called my detective acquaintance and told him what Gabriel had said. I don't know if it was just him doing his job, or the fact that our kids went to the same school, but he had Gabriel apprehended. The police searched his apartment. There wasn't any dismembered body in there, thank God. Even though they found nothing nefarious, I was relieved that they had taken Gabriel in for evaluation, and I felt as though a weight had been lifted off of my shoulders. He was in custody now, and I was sure that the severity of his mental illness would be obvious, and that he would get the help that he needed.

A few days later I received a call from an attorney working for the prosecution. There was going to be a civil proceeding to determine if Gabriel should be committed. I was going to be the plaintiff and Gabriel the defendant, and the kicker was that he had chosen to defend himself. He and I would now be adversaries. This is not what I intended at all, but now I had to see it through, for Gabriel's safety, for everyone's.

I cleared my day, canceled my appointments and surgeries for the day of the hearing and reported to the courthouse. The ancient building, with its echoing hallways and metal detectors, strangely reminded me of my old high school. I wandered down the hall looking at every doorway and the listing of each trial that was framed on the wall next to the door. Eventually I found the actual courtroom where the proceedings regarding Gabriel were to be conducted. The room was paneled in wood, ceiling to floor, like the old law school library that I used to spend Friday nights studying in. There were many more people inside the courtroom than I had expected, but it was still mostly empty. I sat toward the back of the small crowd and settled in for what I was sure was going to be a long, strange day.

Suddenly, I had a sick feeling. I began to sweat, and I could feel a sense of panic emerging. How horrible that it had come to this. I should have known that it was not possible for a man of his intelligence and ambitions to simply sit by and watch the world turn. My carefully constructed facade had been slowly crumbing and now the whole thing was coming down. I had always feared that it would end badly, and it was about to

The judge came into the courtroom. That distracted me and I began to calm down. Then I realized that the judge looked familiar. I never forget a face; he had been a patient of mine. I had performed surgery on this judge. Although it had only been a few months since I had seen him in my office, he didn't seem to acknowledge or remember me. *Weird coincidence? Isn't that a conflict of interest? Who forgets the name of their surgeon, especially if the plaintiff, with that very name, in your courtroom, is in fact a surgeon?*

For some unknown reason, the judge wanted to conceal our patient-doctor relationship. I was sure that he knew exactly who I was, but for some unknown reason he wanted to conceal that knowledge so that he could rule on this case. Why would he do that? He was up to something, but I couldn't figure out what it was. I considered approaching him and foiling whatever his plan was. I could have said something, but I knew that it would only delay the proceedings. I kept waiting for him to remember who I was, to give me a signal. I thought for sure that I saw a slight smirk on his face when he looked my way, but when I nervously waved at him, he never acknowledged me. I kept my mouth shut, but I also kept my eye on that judge. I didn't trust him.

I sat on one of the wooden benches looking around. The scene was almost like a church. The room was cavernous, with a high ceiling. The courthouse building itself was a beautiful Roman style with massive cement columns along its front. I had driven by the building many times growing up in that town. My whole life I had seen it from the freeway or when traveling on the bus down Wisconsin Avenue on my way to the university.

It was an impressive building—a beautiful structure on the outside, but inside it had been filled in past decades with dated furnishings from the 1960's and 1970's. Some of the original decor remained. There were dark wooden benches running along the corridors and marble floors, cast iron pendant light fixtures with alabaster bowls hanging from the high hallway ceilings. Even though it was September and there was no air conditioning, the hallways were surprisingly cool, like my old high school building had been. Buildings like that seem to always stay cool, like caves.

Gabriel was escorted into the courtroom under guard, but not shackled or cuffed. After all, he was not a criminal. He looked okay. I had guessed that he had been psychologically evaluated and put on medications. He seemed calm, but not sedated. He didn't see me among the other people seated in the courtroom. In the crowd I felt invisible. I wondered who these people were. How could anyone be interested in our pathetic little disaster? Missing from the attendants was Gabriel's family. I thought that maybe they were exhausted and in survival mode. Perhaps they had given up and disowned Gabriel.

The hearing started, and the judge explained to Gabriel that he had been accused of making threats against me and my family, and that he would decide whether Gabriel was a threat to himself or others. He spoke to Gabriel as if he was a child.

"Do you understand why you are here?"

"Yes sir... I mean yes, Your Honor, I think so."

"And what is it that you think you are accused of?"

"I have been told that someone who used to be my friend says that he was afraid that I might try to hurt him or his family."

"So, you understand that the charges against you are serious?"

"I guess I wouldn't be here if they weren't?"

The judge bristled. "Are you certain you wish to proceed without benefit of counsel?

"Gabriel nodded. "Yes sir... I mean Your Honor. I haven't hurt anyone."

"Well, that's one reason we are here," the judge said. "Do you understand that the charges could result in you being detained indefinitely or restricted to where you can go and who you may have contact with?"

"I think so, Your Honor. . . but I don't think that will happen because I haven't—"

The judge cut him off. "Let's proceed."

After the initial statements by the judge and the prosecuting attorney, there was a brief recess, after which, I was called into the courtroom. I walked down the long aisle between the jury box and the spectators. I was put on the witness stand. I took the oath. The judge, still pretending not to have ever seen me before, instructed me. I looked him in the eyes, like *what are you trying to pull here*, but I didn't see any reaction from him. The prosecutor quickly established my relationship with Gabriel and the threats he had made against my children and me.

Gabriel began his questioning. It was horrible. It was like a bad play. He paced back and forth in front of the raised witness stand asking me all kinds of questions that seemed disorganized and random. The judge tried to keep him on track, and he finally got to the gist of the matter.

"Now, you claim that I told you to come over to my apartment and clean up a mess, and that then I said that I was going to chop you up in my meat grinder, isn't that so?"

"Yes, that's correct."

"But you're a surgeon, aren't you?"

"Yes."

"Well, don't you think that you're much more capable and likely to chop someone up in a meat grinder than me?"

I remember looking at the judge and thinking, *is this really going on?* I remember the judge's blank stare. I started to have this weird feeling that maybe I was the one who was deranged and paranoid. There were a few follow up questions from the prosecutor about the timing of the threats, Gabriel's mental health history, and the episodes of paranoia I had witnessed over the years. The rest of the questions seemed to be a blur. The prosecutor also called medical experts who had treated Gabriel over the years, and also produced evidence of him being institutionalized. Gabriel tried to convolute the testimony of the experts, but the judge would have none of it. The hearing was over by noon.

I was instructed to wait outside the courtroom while the judge, the prosecutor, and Gabriel discussed the court's decision. I went out into the hallway. I sat on one of those dark wooden benches that lined each side of the wide corridor. Professional looking people walked back and forth. Uniformed police and other uniformed employees shuffled by. I looked at their guns as they passed by me. The guns looked much bigger and heavier than I thought they would. It seemed that it would be so easy for someone to just reach out and grab one of those heavy handguns right out of its holster.

Time passed slowly. The longer that I waited, the more anxious I was getting. I was wondering what was going on in that courtroom. What was Gabriel doing or saying? What about that judge? What was he saying? I was angry that I wasn't allowed to be in there, to make sure that the facts were accurate, to correct the details, to make sure that they were getting it right.

One of the assistants to the prosecutor came out into the corridor and told me that there was going to be a lunch break. She said that the proceedings would then reconvene for the verdict, and I should be back in ninety minutes. I had no appetite, so I just sat there on the wooden bench. I imagined that I was back in church; the people walking through the corridor were like the priest and the altar boys doing the stations of the cross. I wanted to kneel and pray a little. I wondered if they'd let me, if I did that, or would everyone laugh at me, or maybe put me on trial? Instead, I just closed my eyes. I tried to imagine the smell of that incense that the priests used to burn, and they would swing it back and forth—the smell and the silence. After a long wait, nobody ever came out to call me back into the courtroom. I walked over to the door and opened it to check. The courtroom was empty. Confused, I turned down the long hallway and made my way home.

Two days later the prosecutor called me to tell me that Gabriel had been committed. I remember feeling relieved at first. Then I hung up the phone and I cried.

I went back to work the next day, back to my routine. My one comfort was the hope that Gabriel was going to get some real help, and, at least for a little while, we were all safe, including him.

Three days later I received another call from the prosecutor's office, this time notifying me that Gabriel was going to be released the following day, and that I should take whatever precautions I felt necessary.

"I thought that you said he had been committed, indefinitely."

"That's correct sir. He was committed... to outpatient therapy, but don't worry, they will be keeping a close eye on him."

CHAPTER 22
A Night in Tunisia

Art Blakey and The Jazz Messengers, "*A Night in Tunisia*" 11:15. 1963 Blue Note release. It has everything that I love about jazz. It's Hard bop. It's perfection, the pinnacle of jazz. It's frightening in its build. They're shouting from a sand dune somewhere. Its power and brains and art. Such a beautiful and rare combination that it is almost intimidating in its chaos. This one is the primal power of Art Blakey and Wayne Shorter and Lee Morgan. They would all go their separate ways after that night in Tunisia. Blakey would stay on as the foundation of the Jazz Messengers, Shorter would replace Coltrane in the new Miles Davis Quintet, and the prodigy—the young Lee Morgan—he would be shot down by his wife.

"You seem agitated Michael. Perhaps we should take the rest of the day off so that you can rest?" Dr. Sanders inquired.

I was so wired at that point that I simply ignored her question.

"Dr. Sanders, after the court case, things kept happening to me that I couldn't understand. I felt like I was escaping gravity somehow."

"Can you give me some examples of that?" she asked.

"Yeah, I can. I was driving with my children in the car, on the freeway. This guy pulled up alongside me. I looked over at him. My kids looked over at him. He put his fingers to his head like a gun and just smiled at me. My daughter said, "What is going on daddy?" If she hadn't said that, I swear to God I would have thought it was only in my head, in my mind. I told her that I didn't know what was going on."

"Have you had other episodes that proved to be confusing? Please tell me more."

"Okay. I had been driving home one day when I saw a hitchhiker. Nobody picks up hitchhikers anymore, right, but I do from time to time. He went into the back seat, and that made me nervous. We made small talk. I was driving south on the sixteenth street viaduct, and he started telling me how he had killed a woman and thrown her over the viaduct into the Menominee River. I pulled over and, without turning off the engine, jumped out of the car, leaving the door open. I yelled at him until he got out and wandered away. I stood there looking at the car, with its doors open, engine running, me in the road, the guy walking backward just looking at me.

Another time, I was grocery shopping, and an old man came up to me with a box of prepared food. He asked me if I would buy it for him. I looked at the price, five dollars, and I said sure, but told him he'd have to wait because I had some groceries to get. I went about buying my groceries, my coffee beans, my chips and scones. I was so caught up in my silly little world that I forgot that this starving, skinny, old guy was waiting to eat his food. When I was checking out, he was waiting there by the exit, just looking at me. I pushed my cart to the doors and handed him his meal. He didn't thank me. He asked me for a ride home. Again, I said sure. He said very few words as he directed me through the downtown streets on the rough side of town. It was winter and it was dusk and most of the streetlights were out. There were no leaves on the trees. The houses were either boarded up or torn down. There weren't many that appeared to have anyone living in them. I remember wondering where he could possibly be living, here among the damage. Suddenly he loudly said, "Here!"

I pulled over. He got out and leaned back into the car. Again, he didn't thank me, but told me to drive like hell and not to stop.

Another time there was a carjacking that I witnessed on one of my neighborhood streets. I made a left turn right through a red light and I chased them through downtown while arguing with the 911 operator. "Stop chasing the carjackers sir," the dispatcher implored me."

"Do you think you were out looking for trouble," Dr. Sanders asked.

"Maybe. I guess. I'd run at night, through the worst parts of town, looking for confrontation, for punctuation, for salvation. I'd fantasize about strangling rude awful strangers with piano wire."

"What do you make of that behavior now," the doctor asked.

"When I was doing this stuff, I thought that there was something wrong with me. I knew that on some level, it didn't seem right, but I also thought that maybe there was something wrong with everyone else. Finally, something happened that really messed with my head. After everything that I had done and seen and endured, this event seemed to strike the final blow."

"And what was that?"

No answer. He stopped.

"I can see how upset you are." The doctor said. "I'm here just to listen to you Michael. If you prefer, we can break for the day. If you feel like you would rather keep talking, please continue."

I snapped back from the blurry state of mind I was in and recounted a story for Dr. Sanders.

I remembered walking through the hallways of the surgery department early one morning, before my cases for the day. A call came over the speakers, requesting any available surgeon to come to the ER. This sort of thing was quite unusual because this hospital was not a trauma center. The EMTs knew better than to bring a trauma patient here. Any gunshots that ended up here either walked in on their own, or they were dumped at the front door by their friends in an attempt to save them. The latter was the case here. I was not the surgeon on call for the day, but I was available. My aversion to trauma had not diminished over the years, but now I had a sort of fatalistic mentality. I was almost robotic by this time. Despite the disconnected numbness that was beginning to define me, I still knew that I had a responsibility, an obligation to do my job.

I walked calmly toward the ER, trying to mentally prepare myself. Once again, I figured that maybe, if I walked slowly, there was a chance that some other surgeon would get there before me. I did walk slowly, but not slowly enough. When I arrived in the ER, the nurses quickly directed me to the room. I met the emergency physician. She told me that the patient was fifteen years old, the same age as my son at the time. Then the doctor told me that the boy had been shot in the upper abdomen. He had been awake and conversant upon arrival, but during his evaluation he had suddenly become unresponsive. I approached the boy's room and pulled back the curtains. I paused to see this young man, lifeless. I remember his limbs splayed out like a cartoon figure as nurses performed CPR.

The ER doc told me that the exit wound was in the upper back, above the diaphragm. That the bullet had passed through the chest and probably resulted in an injury to either the heart, lungs, or what we call the great vessels—the aorta or pulmonary vessels. In my training, there was only one option, one intervention—to open the chest right there, in the ER, in hopes of being able to clamp across the injured vessel, put a finger in a hole, or suture it closed and save his life. I had to think fast. I looked around at the meager supplies available to me. Next, I did something that even I didn't know was possible; I made an incision just below the nipples all the way across the chest, then took some heavy scissors, the ones usually employed to cut off the clothes of trauma patients, and I cut between the ribs and across the sternum horizontally to open the chest like a clam shell. When I did that, the dark purple blood erupted like a fire hydrant out of the boy. There was so much blood that I couldn't see anything else. There were no transfusions available. There was one feeble suction tube and canister. There was a volcano of blood. I tried to stop it with my hands—to clamp something blindly to slow it enough to find where it was coming from. Humans only have about five liters of blood. It didn't take long for that volcano to spew those five liters out onto the floor and for that boy to die, right there, with my hands in his chest.

I remember a nurse in the room telling me how I was her hero—because I had come in there all cool and cracked this kid's chest with nothing more than a pair of scissors that you could pull out of your kitchen drawer.

"I didn't do shit for that kid." I had said, and I staggered down the hall. I would never return to that ER. I still remember that boy's face and his limbs and his blood.

"I'm telling you this, Dr. Sanders, because most surgeons would forget that. They would go home at the end of the day and sleep soundly at night. I envy them. I cannot forget it. I know that I won't ever forget it, and that does not make me any better than them. In fact, it may make me worse."

"I know about that event—the boy dying in the ER. The administrator at your hospital told me about the boy's death, and how you quit shortly after. She said that the boy was trying to steal a car before school and was shot by the owner. This really affected you."

Dr. Sanders and I sat quietly for a while as I tried to bring order to a series of thoughts ricochetting in my head.

"I have been reading some of your writing. Your wife gave this to me. I hope that you are alright with that."

I paged through the notebook on my lap. "Tell me, is this story about what happened in that neighborhood?"

Dr. Sanders spoke to me so softly. She looked at me as if she was looking straight into my head. She handed me the notebook. It was mine. It contained the things that I had written down, to help me deal—to help me vent a little. I had nobody, no one who I could talk about these things with. I mean, I could have told anyone I suppose, but nobody could see it, or hear it, or even care about it, even if they tried. I read the words, my words, but they seemed unfamiliar:

THE BIRD FLIES *as it wishes and where it chooses. It soars high above, dives, or perches on a lamppost. As the crow flies, or the hawk, or vulture—through suburbs, neighborhoods, downtown, uptown, alleys and boulevards—it's all the same to the bird. I too traverse these places. My course is not straight. It is not chosen. I wander, a search without an objective, in search of nothing more than today, and then tomorrow.*

It was on such a path that this man, this lost doctor, met the child and his mother. Three days prior, a fifteen-year-old boy had died in my arms. His blood so quickly left his body to pool on the floor as to seem intentional, escaping its confinement, only to be stepped upon and later mopped up like any other mess.

Life goes that quickly. Everyone resumed their own lives and jobs, as did I, but I could not stop seeing that boy's face, beautiful and brown, but dead now, arms and legs in disarray, only how the dead lay.

I drift into anger. I was angry with this young boy who wakes in the morning and decides to steal a car. I was angry with a man whose car is worth more than that life. I was angry with a place where these choices have to be made, and angry with the world for putting me there too, powerless to change any of it. I wept and clenched my teeth and my fists. I cursed a god that sits by.

In the days that followed, I became withdrawn, like a bird floating on the wind, too distracted to even move my wings. I was tossed about without intention. A destructive fervor was building. "If our god does not care, why should I? You fool! In the end you can't hurt God. You can't get back at God." The anger turns to bitterness. You hover and glide from place to place, through the neighborhoods. From that height you can see things. The emptiness has left you open, able now to see.

I was coasting through one such day, through one such neighborhood, where the houses lean on one another, where the time of day and the day of the month and the month of the year conspire to create a perfectly empty shade of gray—the color of dirt and cement, with boarded windows blocking any view in, or out.

I was lulled into this blur of sirens and horns and helicopter blades. This white noise was the wind on which I floated, through this late autumn afternoon, among the long shadows and dappled light. Down the street I drove. My eye caught the movement of an animal in the road. As the distance between us closed, it was clear that the stray was actually a child, barely old enough to shuffle down this street. I stopped in my tracks. This typically busy street was now completely empty, but for this beautiful little boy in his pajamas. As he shuffled by my car, his left arm trailing along my drivers' door, a smile came across his face. He looked up into my eyes and continued down the road.

Momentarily jarred from flight, I considered the possibility that I had imagined this scene. When I glanced into my rear view to see the child continuing on, I leaped out of the car in pursuit. He giggled as I swept him up. His skin was beautiful and brown, his hair in neat cornrows, and his face close to mine. When I asked him where he lived, a smile and dimples was the response.

I held him close and safe, turning slowly in the middle of the street. My car, with its engine still running and the door open, sat one block away. I scanned the gray houses, asleep on their feet, for an open door, or a frantic mother. Nothing.

As I held this soft gift in my arms, turning slowly in a circle, in the road, I lost track of gravity for a few moments. I wanted to help this one in the way that I couldn't help the other. I will save this one, this one, the clean smell, smiling, hand to my cheek.

When I awoke from this weightlessness, the street was no longer empty. It had become a parade of cars in both directions. With the child in my arms, I stood in the middle. "Are you okay?" "Do you need any help?" "Is that your child?" "Hey, what you doing with that kid?"

The oddity of this picture, the bird of prey with wings wrapped *around this helpless creature, had jarred the neighborhood awake. His footie-covered feet softly and playfully kicked me. I was also more alert now. I asked him once again, "Where do you live?" Part of me was hoping and knowing that he could not speak. I turned and made my way through the stationary line of vehicles, with windows opened and angry mouths moving silently as I passed each, toward my car, engine running, door opened. "I will save you," I murmured.*

As I leaned into the car to put the child down, a voice halted me. It called out a name or a command. I abruptly straightened and turned. On the sidewalk perpendicular to my car, a woman was coming down the street, wearing a nightgown only, without concern for the cold. With no rush, she smoothly landed in front of me. Her eyes looked calmly into mine. I held the child out to her, and she took him in her arms. There was no expression or change in her gaze. "He autistic. He just runs out sometime."

She turned and left. They both looked back at me—the smile and the dimples still. The mother's eyes were saying something too. There was something sad but comforting in those eyes. They seemed to be saying, "Thanks for trying, but you don't need to save this one."

I returned to the car and closed the door. Uncertain for how long, I sat there and stared straight ahead. There were no horns, no sirens, no angry voices, just the empty street, and me.

SHE HAD ASKED me to read it aloud to her, but I couldn't. I brushed through it quickly and said, "Yes. That's pretty much how it happened— or maybe I imagined it all. I really can't tell anymore. You know what's funny—I went back to that neighborhood a few days later, to drop my son off at school in the morning. I saw a puppy wandering around in the bushes in front of one of the houses, then it ran across the street to another house. I pulled my car over again because I thought that maybe the puppy might be the spirit of the dead boy. I wanted to save the puppy. Obviously, nobody was watching it, or cared about it. Before I could get out of my car, a guy came out of the house in boxers. He looked like Gabriel. He glared at me for a second, then he picked up the dog and took it inside. I remember thinking, *What is wrong with you man? Pull yourself together. Don't let them see this. Don't tell anyone about this.*

"Do you think that it really had been Gabriel?" the doctor asked. "Did your son see him?"

"No. I had already dropped my son off. I don't think that it was him. Maybe it was. It's just that all those weird events, all random and unconnected, led me to the point where I found myself ready, ready to confront it all, to yell at God and at the devil and anyone else who kept fucking with me, ready to be violent even or just to end it all. It all led to this, but at the time I never knew it, never understood why. You see, God had put me here, now he damn well had to figure out what to do with me. So, he does this, and he does that. It all seems random to us, but it's not."

CHAPTER 23
Point of Departure

"Dedication," the fourth track, 6:44. The 1964 Blue Note release, *Point of Departure*. Andrew Hill on piano, Kenny Dorham—trumpet, the atonal Eric Dolphy on alto sax. Joe Henderson, Richard Davis and Anthony Williams round out the group. To me, each musician on this track sounds as though they are lamenting. It's a collaboration of the freshest sounds in jazz—the avant-garde, yet, here they are solemn, restrained. Respect for the past, for the people.

Dr. Sanders noticed me drifting in and out of myself during our last conversation. I was losing track of what I was saying, my thoughts fragmented. Some I recognized and others not.

"Michael, are you with me?"

No response.

"Are you with me?" she repeats.

"Michael's not here. I don't see him," I say.

"Then, I must be speaking to Gabriel."

She had almost begun to feel as though she was speaking to two people at the same time. She decided to take a leap of faith, in an effort to draw one of them out. She had been trained in this technique, but before today, she had never had the opportunity to try it.

"Well, I am certainly glad to meet you finally," I say. I feel like I know this kind lady, but I'm not sure how or to what extent. She feels trustworthy.

"Can you tell me a little about yourself and about Michael, about your history and the nature or your relationship?"

"Let's see, how can I summarize Michael? It's easy, but it's not... you know? He was alright. I mean, he was a little uptight you see... like hyper-focused all the time. He couldn't just be. He had trouble just letting go sometimes. He didn't know how to be alone with himself or how to be lonely. I could teach him something about that. You know what else? He was afraid of being poor, you know? He had to succeed. He had to get out. I'm like, where you going? There's no getting out."

"You were close though, right?"

"Yeah, we were close."

"Can you tell me anything more?"

"Yeah. I can tell you a ton more. I've been waiting to talk to you. See, he never lets me talk to anyone, so I got lots to say. I've been watching you. I can see in your eyes that you care about him, just like I do, but I'm here to warn you. Don't let yourself be drawn in by him. Don't get too close to him, because the minute that he doesn't need you, you're gone."

"What do you mean by *gone*?"

"It's always been just me and him, me and him. He's always liked it that way. He didn't like if I started to get somewhere in life, like meet a girl, get a job, make some friends, get into medical school. He'd put an end to that in a hurry... undermine me, sabotage things. He always just wanted it to be me and him against this shitty world. You know what the problem with that is? He made it out, or at least he thought that he did. That's the problem, right? I mean, how can it be me and him against the world when now it's really just me against the world? He thought that he had made it out, and I'd helped him. Now, here I was, here to hang out with him when he needed me, go to his big house when he wanted me to. Yeah, he'd buy me drinks and burgers and sometimes even girls. But you know what? I wouldn't even thank him, just to fuck with him."

"Why? Wasn't he your friend?"

"Yes. He was my friend! He was my best friend, and my only friend, and I loved him. But he left me. Can you see that?"

"He's told me a lot about you. It's clear to me that he really cares about you. He always has."

"I told you to watch out for that. Don't you get it? He didn't really need me anymore. All of the sudden I became invisible, and let me tell you, there's nothing worse than being invisible."

"So Gabriel, do you simply disappear and reappear at times?"

I laugh. "You're supposed to be smart. I'm speaking figuratively, you know? I meant that he no longer *wanted* to see me. That's how I became invisible, and that's when I started to realize something else. I started to realize that he had *my* life. He had stolen *my* life. He was living *my* life. That should have been *my* life. Instead, I was stuck in this limbo. When we were young it was different. We were both moving forward, together, listening to jazz, talking every day, studying, stickin' it to The Man.

We had big plans. But, at some point he turned away from me. I tried to find a way back in, but he only wanted me in that role because that's what worked for him. But you know what? It didn't work for me anymore. He turned on me. I wasn't going to have that. Sure, he helped me through some tough times, but nobody's had it tougher than me—certainly not that weak-ass punk. I am the survivor here. I have been rejected by my father, and my mother, and my sisters. I was not about to be set aside by this guy. I had been in the background for too long. I have something to offer. I have brains and looks and skills. I couldn't be kept down like that. I had always been tougher than him. I was going to turn the tables. That's when I decided to take my life back, but to do that, I would have to take his."

"So that's when you decided to end his life?"

"Well, it's not that simple."

CHAPTER 24
Of Two Minds

Hank Mobley's "Split Feelin's," 4:55. Blue Note, 1960, from the release *Soul Station*. It sounds like a basketball bouncing down the street—like the kid missed the shot and the ball bounced on for blocks. Basketballs don't care about cars, or anything.

I AM ALONE NOW. The doctor left. Our exchange has left me feeling alienated, somehow, even vulnerable. One good thing, though. That pesky Detective Roman is no longer showing up much, and I was glad about that. I didn't trust him. There was something in his tone that seemed patronizing. Despite my openness about everything to this point, I felt as though he thought I was hiding something, being dishonest.

I've known for a while that something was up. Although I'm in a medical hospital, there was a guard stationed outside my door. There was also a nurse or nurse's aide in my room at all times. I am never left alone and not allowed to leave the room or shave myself. I was told by the staff that it was for my protection. I guess that should have been believable enough, given what had happened to me.

Dr. Sanders is my constant. She should be showing up. As I lay and wait, I think about some of what we have discussed. I remember some of our talks, but there are lapses. My mind dashes to my early days at the lipo clinic in California, something we have discussed before, but in how much detail I do not recall.

I remember following the proctor closely, but not too close. He walked very quickly and would make sudden changes in his direction causing him to bump into someone too close. This would result in some exaggerated gesture of frustration and annoyance. *Better to not follow too closely.*

From the beginning I had a bad feeling. It was almost as if I had been cast into some strange form of hell—a place where I would relive my past experiences, but in a bizarre new setting. In the early weeks, I was told not to speak to the patients, or to anyone, unless I was told to. When operating, he would slap my hands, or even grab them if he didn't think that I was doing something correctly. All of this had an unpleasant nostalgia to it, reminding me of all the years of abuse that I had endured in training and all of the egocentric asses that I had tolerated in Milwaukee and Pittsburgh. Now, here I was in California with some two-bit surgeon trying to intimidate me, trying to build himself up by knocking someone else down. It was infuriating. It took everything I had to hold it together, to focus. I felt like just letting loose and telling him, *"Hey man, I'm the guy who can operate with both hands at the same time. I can remove every goddamn organ in the body and put it back right where it belongs. I'm the guy who can cut open a dying teenager's chest with kitchen scissors. Don't you fucking tell me how to suck fucking fat, and don't you ever touch my hand."*

Although those words swam about in my mind continuously, I kept it inside. My training at the lipo clinic was progressing ahead of schedule. I had always been technically skilled and able to put my head down and keep my mouth shut and do the work. Despite my initial bravado, I quickly fell back into the good soldier role that I had been so accomplished at, those many years earlier. I was ashamed at how quickly I had capitulated.

The patients were awake during these procedures. To make this possible, the anesthetic fluid was mixed with the bags of IV fluid.

Epinephrine was mixed in also, to cause vasoconstriction and minimize blood loss. Several tiny incisions were made and then the fluid was infused into the fat layer using a long pulsating probe. The probe was narrow and flexible, to get around corners. There was skill required to do this properly, and with as little pain as possible. This was the relatively low-key portion of the case. There would be small talk with the patient, music playing. The proctor would tell jokes to distract the patient from their discomfort. The patient would be turned from side to side until all of the areas were addressed, and all of the IV bags were emptied. This typically required about forty minutes, then it would be time to begin the suctioning.

The proctor would lay the device on the patient and turn it on so they could feel it vibrate. "Don't be afraid of this," he would say.

Approximately five liters of liquefied fat is the maximum volume that could be removed safely in one setting; more than that could cause shifts in blood pressure or consciousness that were dangerous. As each liter container was filled with liquid fat, a nurse would parade it past the patient and tell them to look at what's been accomplished so far. Patients would stop grimacing briefly when they realized the result of it all.

This was sweaty work, very physical, always moving, pumping, sweeping, making feathering motions, the whole time talking to the patient in an effort to distract them. The nurses in the room constantly moved as well, keeping track of the volumes infused and suctioned, changing canisters, writing the numbers down, calling out volumes. Early on, I would only watch, but as the weeks went on, I was allowed to do more and more of the procedures. The proctor started to realize that I was not the usual trainee, and he started to let me go. After several weeks of training, he would leave the room and return to assess my results.

Although my technique was progressing ahead of schedule, my attitude had been going in the other direction. The more of this that I did, the more disenchanted I became. I was sucking fat. It was simply maximally invasive psychotherapy, its only goal being to make patients feel better about themselves. I had been trained to treat people who needed treatment, people who were sick or dying, who had to have surgery. Telling jokes and singing to patients with loud pounding pop music in the background was giving me headaches. I was starting to feel that my brain wasn't right. I could feel it tingle.

I tried not to think about what I was doing there. I tried to focus on why I was there in the first place—the money. Living in California was expensive, and I still had a lot of debt. This gig was a sure thing though, sure money, but it was pure crazy. *Was this all part of some plan?* The truth is that I had always had a plan, an end game that provided me with the strength to turn the other cheek and to continue toward that end—an end that would make it all worthwhile and provide me and the people I love with security and happiness.

As it turned out, I would have been better off working that factory job like my dad. He did have some happy times, and that job provided for his family—the people he loved. Nothing is forever. Nothing stays the same. His job was never secure, and he was reminded of that every time a nearby factory went out of business or was bought by foreign investors. He had no control. At any moment, his whole world could all be pulled out from under him. He was also haunted by regrets and ambition. Perhaps that is it—ambition; it's like a drug that, in the right amount is inspiring, but a little too much of it makes you hate your life.

I was no different. I was so afraid of that regret that I did everything I could to ensure that I would never experience it. Whatever I did, it didn't seem to change who I was. Hell, I was just a machinist's son from Milwaukee. I had no more control over my life than he had over his. I never felt like I belonged back there, but I didn't belong here either. Maybe I don't belong anywhere.

In the end, that's why I formed this plan—this money maker. It would solve all my problems. All I had to do was sell my soul. Now, after the past several weeks, I was fighting the urge to cut and run, from everything. There's a saying in sports that once an athlete starts talking about retirement, in a way, they're already there. I was feeling like that. I had wanted it all at one point, now I didn't want any of it. I was now of two minds about success and fortune. I thought that I knew what was important in life, what success meant. Now I was realizing that success was overrated. Its cost was too steep. Nothing made sense to me anymore. The more I thought about it, the more I realized that I didn't want to fight the battle anymore. I kept remembering a phrase that someone had told me once. *"One should never be of two minds on anything you know. They will live off each other and neither one will survive."*

CHAPTER 25
Serenade to a Cuckoo

Rhsaan Ronald Kirk and his quartet, 1965 "Serenade to A Cuckoo" on *I Talk With the Spirits.* The multi-instrumentalist, blind from the age of two, modified instruments to allow himself to play several at the same time. It's what the sounds in his head required of the universe. Perhaps the most beautiful instrument is his own voice, which you can hear on several of the tracks.

MY MIND GOES dark for a while and when I come around Dr. Sanders is still with me, and I could count on her being there every day.

"Welcome back," she says.

"In our last visit you told me about these strange events that were happening to you and how you felt you were losing control of things. Did that begin to happen after you testified against Gabriel in court? And is that why you left Milwaukee and moved to California?" the doctor asked. Did you no longer feel safe after Gabriel was released?"

"For a long while I was looking over my shoulder. At the same time, I was feeling the emptiness of having lost my best friend again, and in such a distressing and painful manner. There was also guilt that I was feeling. I felt as though I had somehow betrayed him."

"I understand that, Michael. But did you feel safe?"

"We discussed the situation with our kids, and they were made aware that they had to keep away from him if they ever saw him. Of course, this was frightening for them, but after a while, when he didn't show up or bother us, the anxiety and vigilance waned."

I told her how I had tried reinventing myself. I focused on making positive changes in my life. I quit smoking. I began to get healthy, running, cycling. I was feeling good. Maybe a year or two had passed. Then it started happening. Gabriel started showing up. It seemed as though I was seeing him everywhere I went. Once, I was at a stoplight and he walked past me in the crosswalk. It was just a coincidence, right? He didn't look at me, just walked by, but these things were happening so often that it couldn't be simply a matter of chance.

Sometimes he'd come to our house. He'd go to the side door and ring the bell. My wife would tell me not to answer it. A couple times I went to the kitchen drawer to get a knife. And, on a couple occasions, in the end, I opened the door.

"Why would you do that, Michael. Weren't you afraid he might attack you or your family?"

"I guess that I had a kind of fatalistic sense about the whole thing at that point. I figured if he's going to shoot me then let's get on with it. He'd stare at me and say something like 'are we good.' I'd lie and say 'Yeah, sure, we're good.' Then he would vanish."

"Were there any specific interactions you had that gave you concern about your safety?"

I thought about that question for a minute. "Yes, yes there was."

It was near Christmas and there was snow on the ground. I was looking out of an upstairs window down to our front lawn and I saw him walking up the street. He was completely in camouflage. He was wearing a large backpack. He turned up the steps that led to our front door, but he stopped there. He took off the backpack and set it on the concrete. Right then, a neighbor of mine was driving down the street and witnessed this. He stopped in front of our house. He rolled down his window and said something to Gabriel, asking him what he was doing, I think. Gabriel waved him off, saying that he was a friend of mine. I could hear the muffled exchange through the closed windows. I ran downstairs to warn my wife. Then we both watched him through the downstairs windows. He was crawling around in the snow, placing sticks in the bushes in front of the house amidst the string Christmas lights. He was speaking to somebody. I could see his lips moving, but I couldn't hear anything. He was very purposeful, and it took quite a while. Then he went back to his pack, looked around, and walked off. After a few minutes I thought that maybe I should have talked to him. So, I got into my car and drove around the neighborhood looking for him, but he was gone.

This was around the time that all of the other events I described began to occur. I was looking at life differently. I was doing all this running and these endurance events—self-imposed suffering. Nobody cares that you can run a marathon or climb a mountain or swim five miles in frigid water. Nobody cares, and why should they? I made friends in that arena, but they were all a different version of myself, lost and chasing something that they would never catch.

Even my brothers and sisters and my mother could not relate to me, although they all really tried to. My neighbors and friends—everyone—were drifting away from me.

"I always thought it was them, Dr. Sanders, but now I realize that it was me that was drifting. It wasn't anybody's fault, not mine or theirs. I was just a strange individual. I had been created this way and placed in the wrong world—a place where I couldn't exist like everyone else... the wrong one. At least that's how I see it now, but at that time, I was still trying to figure it out, to make it work."

All of these things happening simultaneously had created quite a storm in my mind. I was behaving recklessly. My friends and family could see it, but they didn't really know what to say to me.

"I think in some instinctual way I knew that I needed to escape, like jumping out of a runaway train only moments before it crashes. That's what I was feeling. That's why we decided to move."

CHAPTER 26
I'm Left Alone

"I'm Left Alone," by the Mal Waldron Trio, featuring Jackie McLean, on the Bethlehem label, 6:05. It was written by Billie Holiday and Mal Waldron, her pianist, on a plane from New York to San Francisco. She said that the song was the story of her life. Jackie's saxophone, always a favorite of mine, usually reminds me of an air raid siren, and everything that comes with that. In contrast, here he is drowning and haunting. Mal's piano seems to be begging Billie not to go. It's like a quiet conversation between friends. But no, she will go. She would soon die from complications of liver failure, the result of decades of self-medicating. It was July 1959, only five months after this dedication and plea was recorded.

From Detective Roman's interviews with liposuction nurses and other staff:

For months the doctor had been declining, I mean in his performance on the job. He had stopped interacting with us much, only minimally. He became slower in his work. Management wasn't happy with his production. Then there was a point when he began talking to himself at work, sometimes during the procedures. He wasn't speaking loud enough for any of us to understand what he was saying, just mumbling kinda, but everyone noticed it, even the patients. That's when I had to report him to the director. I felt sorry for him, I really did. He is a good man, and I had no idea what was going to happen to him now, but I knew that he needed help. I knew that he was stressing me out, me and everyone else who was working with him, and I knew that they were going to let him go soon.

Someone, or maybe it was several people, reported me to the director, who summoned me. I was stunned and embarrassed. I wasn't completely aware of my behavior. What I did know was that I was distracted and worried that Gabriel had found me.

"When did you know that Gabriel was here in California?" Dr. Sanders asked. "How did you find out?"

"I really didn't know. I just had a sense, like a feeling of unease, you know? I tried to convince myself that I was imagining it. I would notice gates ajar, my car vandalized—like silly little things, like tiny signals he was sending me. He wouldn't break the window of my car, but he'd pick the lock and mess everything up inside, and just leave the door slightly ajar. I'd go out to empty the garbage in the evening and the bins would all be backward. At night, when I was lying in bed, I could see shadows moving outside the curtains. I knew that I wasn't dreaming because the dogs would bark."

There was a period of silence, then she asked me if I told my wife about these feelings. I told Dr. Sanders that we had at that point separated and that my kids were in college.

"It was just me... well, and the dogs sometimes. We shared the dogs... took turns.

"Why were you separated from your wife?"

"I'm hard to be with, I think."

"Explain what you mean by that."

"I think a lot."

"That's not a reason."

"Everything means something to me. My mind is going all the time. I guess I'm just repeating what she says to me because I only know how my mind is. Apparently, it's different from other people, at least that's what she says. I believe her though. I didn't always believe her, but I started to realize over the years that maybe she was right. She stuck by me as long as she could. We made this move partly in an attempt to save our marriage. Salvage. But he followed me here, and then she left. She had to save herself, you know?"

"So it's been just you then?"

"Well, she still loves me. I do believe that. My kids love me, but they're away. I get to have the dogs on weekends when I'm not working. But I guess, yeah, most of the time it's just me. That bothered me for a long while, then I started to get used to it. I'm not comfortable being alone. I never have been. It makes me panicky, like I hyperventilate, and I have to get drunk or do something to calm myself."

"So, when Gabriel is around you don't feel alone?"

"Have you ever seen a firefly Dr. Sanders?" I asked.

"No, I don't think that I have. Of course, I've heard of fireflies, but now that I think about it, I don't believe that I actually have ever seen one."

"You would remember it if you'd ever seen one. Are you from California?"

"No, Las Vegas." she said. "Why are you laughing?"

"I just didn't think that anyone was actually from Las Vegas. I always think of it as a place people go to, not a place where one is from. If you're from Las Vegas, then you've definitely not seen any fireflies."

"Why are you asking me about fireflies?"

"You know it's funny, people said I was foolish to move here. They all said that the people in California are crazy. They said there's earthquakes and drought and fires, and it's so expensive. I wouldn't listen to any of them."

"Do you regret your decision? Are you sorry that you came to California?"

"I never realized that there wouldn't be fireflies here. It sounds silly, but with all of the things that people warned me about, all of the warnings that I disregarded, I think that if just one of them would have told me that there weren't any fireflies in California, I might just have stayed where I was."

We both smiled, and I felt my eyes watering a little.

"Tell me about that, Michael. What are you thinking right now?"

"The fireflies are a gift that comes when the day is dying. The end of the day is so bittersweet—the softness of the light from the low-lying sun, the long shadows that seem to give everything a bent appearance, the lazy songs the tired birds sing at the end of the day, so different from the enthusiasm of morning. I used to sit at dusk and watch my two puppies napping under our covered porch. The ceiling fan and the light breeze caused their fur to flutter. Why should such a serene scene be bittersweet? It's only so because I know that it isn't real. I know that it isn't mine, really. I cannot pay for what I have created here, this peaceful place is a mirage. Mentally, physically, spiritually, I cannot pay for it anymore, in tears and blood. It would have been better had I never seen it. And soon, it will all be taken from me, and then, when the shadows get long, I will remember that place and that day, and I will cry to myself, for I will surely be alone then."

We sat in silence for a few moments before I continued.

"It seems ridiculous now. I thought that I could start fresh here—reinvent myself. The truth is that I miss my wife, and my kids. I miss my family back home, and I miss my friends and my old neighbors. If I saw any one of them right now, you'd have to pull me off, because I would just hug them and not let go. Those relationships, those friendships, to me they are like the glow of those fireflies—magical, but too brief. It's taken for granted and then you've lost it. I wish that I would have known the last time I saw a firefly it would be the last time."

"I don't know Michael. I think you'll probably see one again."
"I don't think that I will."

CHAPTER 27
Love And Hate

The bell tolls. It's "Love and Hate," off *Destination Out*, Blue Note, 1963. It has been said that there is a fine line between love and hate. Jackie McLean on alto, Bobby Hutcherson on Vibes, and Grachan Monchour III trombone. They smooth out those edges man. They erase the line completely.

THE NEXT DAY Dr. Sanders wasn't sure who she'd encounter when she entered Michael's hospital room. She sat across from the bed in her usual chair.

"Doctor, it's about time you showed up."

"Gabriel?"

"That's me."

"Okay then, let's get started. I do have some things I'd like you to help me understand."

"Let's do it, Doc."

"Michael says that you had been hanging around the clinic where he works."

"That's right. I started visiting him at the clinic. At first, I'd just hang around in the parking lot so he'd see me when he got off work."

"Why. I mean you two were estranged, were you not."

"Estranged is a polite way to put it. Cast aside, rejected, told to fuck off is more like it. So, yeah, I showed up out here in sunny California to fuck with him. I had been doing things to freak him out. It was working too."

Where you there to scare him or harm him?"

"I was trying to figure out a way to get into the clinic. I wasn't sure what I was going to do once I got in, but I wanted to get in there. The problem was the security guard. The guard was posted at the front door. There had been burglaries at clinics around town, stealing narcotics, so everybody had a security guard now. I was going to have to think on that for a while."

"Gabriel, how did Michael react when he saw you in the parking lot?"

"Like he'd seen a goddamn ghost. He was freaked. Then I would show up at the grocery store, or I would be on the curb hitchhiking when he'd drive by. That's when he finally acknowledged me. He picked me up when I was hitchhiking. I mean, who picks up hitchhikers, right? Well, he pulled over and I got into the back seat. We just sat there silent for a while, then talking for a while. It was awkward for both of us. It's one thing to play games, but when it came time to talk, it wasn't easy for either of us. Oddly, he seemed kind of happy to see me actually. I wasn't expecting that. He drove me to the library and dropped me off there. I told him I'd be in touch."

"Did you rekindle your friendship?"

"Kind of, but I had my own agenda. Even so, before long we started hanging out again. He was working long hours at that damn clinic and was always wiped out. He had to go to bed early, get up early, but he was basically alone now so we could hang out pretty much whenever he was not working or sleeping."

"Did his wife know that you were back in his life?"

Gabriel laughed out loud. "She was long gone, and no, he didn't tell anyone about me this time."

Gabriel paused and then shifted his weight on the bed. His demeanor softened as did his eyes.

"At first, Gabriel unnerved me. He was showing up everywhere.

"Michael?

"Yes, Dr. Sanders?"

"Where is Gabriel now?"

"How would I know. I'm stuck in this hospital bed. But would you like me to pick up where we had left off?"

"Yes Michael, please do."

"Like I said, my wife left me, and I was very lonely. It made me feel better to have someone around who knew me—who knew my history. Who better than Gabriel? What harm could it do to reconnect with him? Maybe he was better. Maybe it would be an opportunity for me to apologize for the way that things had gone down.

"I picked him up hitchhiking one day. It was weird at first. We talked a little and planned to start hanging out soon. He said that he was sorry for everything. He told me that he was having trouble sleeping. He asked me if maybe I could get some valium or something from my clinic. I said sure."

CHAPTER 28
I Put a Spell on You

Screamin' Jay Hawkins wrote "I Put a Spell on You" in 1956. A drunken, earthy, and sweaty cry to the spirits. It's in desperate defiance that he screams into the night. His voice and words say more than I can ever describe. Nina Simone's 1965 version, on Phillips Records, is haunting, a lush symphony of obsession, punctuated by the stuttering sax of King Curtis.

DR. SANDERS WAS asked by the chair of her department to submit a progress report on her interesting patient that had been recently transferred from the ICU, including any insights she may have gained into the details of his diagnosis as well as suggestions for his long-term treatment plan. Several days passed without any sessions with Michael and Gabriel as Dr. Sanders met with her superiors to discuss her findings.

"**THE PATIENT WAS** becoming weaker. Initially, we all thought that perhaps it was due to the stress of the interviews. He was worried about his coworkers at the clinic. He kept asking about them. I purposely didn't give him any information. I thought it might lead to more details from him.

"I told him that there were some concerning test results, that he had a serious infection affecting his liver, which had already been severely damaged by the gun shot. His blood pressure was getting too low, and he needed to be transferred back to the ICU. I could see a look on his face that I can't quite describe—maybe fear, but no, almost a strange smile. I sensed that we were running out of time. I knew what had happened, but the most important details still had not been disclosed. In order to learn more, I needed to hear it from him."

Dr. Sanders was fascinated by this case. In many ways Michael's presentation was classic for a patient who suffers a psychotic break. He had lived through a very traumatic childhood experience, which often creates mistrust in the young mind. He had spent much of his life in a stressful and isolated environment. He trained for years in a world where high expectations and lack of sleep compounded his stress. In many ways he was very typical of a paranoid, multi-personality disorder. What made him unique was his ability to function long term—to balance his disease and his life, to sustain a marriage and raise children—his ability to build a practice.

Michael could not turn off his illness, so he learned how to live with it as well as he could, Dr. Sanders had concluded. He was able to compartmentalize his life—separate his illness from his job, his family. "I've never seen anyone able to do that before." There were always areas of crossover, but they were subtle and were either accepted or overlooked by those around him. At some level Michael recognized his illness and self-medicated, or at least he tried to. He was able to sustain this complicated choreography for a very long time. Cracks in the armor started to form eventually.

"Each time that happened, he'd change direction. When he ran out of directions, he tried to run," Dr. Sanders reported.

His physical deterioration was something that he could not run away from, and eventually that was the tipping point. Most of his physical problems were real, especially the nerve issues affecting his hands. The only exception was the temporary deafness. Michael's temporary hearing loss was classic conversion disorder, which results from a trauma or severe psychological trigger or stress. It was the result of too many layers. "Likely, the move to California was his trigger."

Before the move he had felt that he was alone, even when surrounded by friends, neighbors, and family. But when he moved across the country he was truly alone. It was the final layer. "As these layers accumulated, he became increasingly fragile, both physically and mentally," she told her colleagues.

"I remember something that he related to me that really emphasized these triggers. We were talking about the horrible environment that doctors in training, and especially surgeons, were forced to endure in the name of education. I had asked him if he felt that these feelings were unique to him.

"No, I'm not alone in this." he told me. Dr. Sanders read aloud from her transcript of that conversation with Michael:

"Just a few months ago I was operating, and during the surgery I was talking with the anesthesiologist. It was the first time that I had heard this from her. She told all of us in the room how she had once been a neurosurgery resident. She had spent four years of medical school and six years residency training to be a neurosurgeon, and then, just before completing her training, she gave it all up and switched to a residency in anesthesiology, a field that she felt was more civilized in its training. She related the traumatic events—the unforgivable and inhumane situations, one after another, imposed upon her by those entrusted to train and educate her—her mentors, her proctors. These experiences are what made her run as fast as she could, to get away from the very thing that she had spent more than a decade pursuing. Each of us in the room—the nurse Cassie, Mackenzie the tech, and me—we all had similar stories. The brutality put upon us, the dehumanizing effects of the training, the goal of which, in the end, is to take care of fellow humans—the care of people. It's sick. It's actually the opposite of what you would expect, and this happens to many of us. Why do we put up with it? Why are we drawn to it? For some reason, we are built this way. We have a need to do this, but the doing of it fucks us, some of us worse than others. Maybe we're the ones who are sick. Maybe we are power hungry or in need of constant gratitude and recognition. There is no doubt that many of the surgeons charged with training us had those issues. It's probably different for each of us and probably some combination of all of those things. One thing is true. It's a profession like no other, and it holds us hostage and prisoner because we have a creed, a responsibility, an obligation, because we can do no different."

Dr. Sanders told her colleagues that at some point during her interviews, the patient began to realize that this was not a crime investigation, or therapy. "On some level he knew that we had figured him out. I think that he was actually relieved to finally have someone to talk to—someone who would listen to him and could try to help."

Dr. Sanders said that she had noticed a change in him. He began opening up more, volunteering details and showing remorse and longing. She said his illness had so many unique characteristics, particularly his obsession with jazz music and the many tormented examples of it. "Jazz music was like a soundtrack to his illness," the doctor concluded. In addition to the music, trains and railroads, ships, boats, and vessels were recurring themes in his stories.

"It occurred to me that he was a uniquely steadfast and loyal person. He desired, and even expected the same from everybody in his life, but he was repeatedly disappointed by most of them. In part, I think that this is why Gabriel came to be. He was a construct that Michael created—one that would not let him down. I wanted to understand the significance of every detail of Gabriel's life—how and why Michael's mind had created this specific and particular person. It was fascinating to me."

Dr. Sanders had interviewed several people in Michael's life—his wife, neighbors, coworkers, and his kids. His wife said Michael would talk about his friend Gabriel but that he had never brought him around. At some point she became suspicious and thought that perhaps he was having an affair and using the Gabriel character as a cover.

His adult children remembered how, when they were younger, he used to set an extra place setting at the dinner table for a possible unexpected guest, but the guest would never arrive. The neighbor who Michael had said saw Gabriel wondering around on the lawn in the snow, told Dr. Sanders that it was actually Michael he had seen.

"As interesting as all of this is, I know that the clock is ticking. It is clear at this point that what is left of Michael's liver is failing. I have been noticing a look of surrender in his eyes, as they have begun to turn progressively yellow with jaundice. The specialists told both of us that his chances of survival without a liver transplant are low. His prognosis is grave. Despite this news, he remains calm. He promised me that he would continue to fight. I encouraged him to persevere like he always has. Perhaps a transplant will become available. If we can save his body, I am convinced that, with proper psychiatric treatment, we can get him back on his feet. He could live a meaningful life. I need some more time with him. Neither of us has any control over that."

CHAPTER 29
Evidence

"Evidence," Steve Lacy and Don Cherry, 4:59, released in 1962. Thelonius Monk composed the tune. Lacy plays the soprano sax, an instrument all but absent from the bop era. Cherry and his trumpet stagger out of the free jazz wilderness of Ornette Coleman to lay down the sizzle and boil it over.

***

FROM DETECTIVE ROMAN'S *interviews with an OR liposuction nurse:*

The doctor's behavior was fairly normal and appropriate initially, but during the second case he seemed to be very much on edge. He didn't talk much. A third patient was prepped and ready. He came bounding into the operating room like he was on something. He had a look and smile on his face that was almost unrecognizable. He began shouting out instructions that made no sense. Patients wear eye masks, like those you wear for sleeping. He leaned over the patient and asked her what her go-to karaoke song was. She thought about it for a few seconds, then he motioned to me to put it on. It was an upbeat pop song. He kept telling the nurse to turn it up louder and louder. The patient was high on Xanax and oxycodone. The two of them were singing along. He had the instruments in his hands up over his head waving them around. The nurse turned and ran out of the room and down the hall to the director's office. He was always on the phone, so she ripped the phone out of his hand and almost pulled him up to his feet by his scrubs. The nurse told him that the doctor had finally lost it. He was behaving dangerously. She told him to call security.

Dr. Sanders decided that it was now or never. She asked me to describe what had happened the day of the shooting.

"The day started out very typically. I was pumping and sucking and sweating. After the first procedure I went into the prep room to get the bags ready for the next one. Gabriel was in there sitting there on a stool with a grin. I was unsettled. I asked him how he had gotten past the guard out front. He smiled strangely at me and said that maybe he was just resourceful, and that I should know this by now.

He laughed at me. Then he started insulting me.

"I think even I could do this." he said. "Why don't you let me do the next one? You're nothing special. Anybody can do this sort of thing."

I told him that he had to leave, that I could get fired for this, or worse, that I had another case to attend to, and when I returned, I didn't want to see him in here—I wanted him gone. I turned and left. I was scared. Gabriel seemed different than the friend that I had known. He seemed maniacal.

I could barely focus on the next procedure. It took a little over two hours. Afterward, with a sense of dread, I burst into the prep room. I thanked God that he had left, but he must not have left. He must have done something to me. I was soaking wet with sweat. It's possible that the combination of the stress and dehydration caused me to pass out. I'm not sure what he did to me, but I lost consciousness. I know that it was him."

"Gabriel? Is this Gabriel?" Dr. Sanders asked.

Gabriel threw his head back and laughed. "That sucker! I told Michael that I was having trouble sleeping. I asked him if he could get me something from the clinic. In true Michael form he came through for me. That was his thing, and I knew it. He couldn't say no to someone who needed him. I knew that. He gave me a bunch of Xanax, along with careful instructions on their safe use. I pretended to be grateful, and I pretended to listen to his instructions.

Michael had once told me jokingly that the security guard outside the front of the clinic loved his high-end coffee. Michael hated that scam. He always made his own coffee. I didn't care one way or the other. I went to that overpriced bullshit Starbucks and got the guard a decaf double tall skinny blah blah blah sweet ass latte and crumbled a handful of the pills in there.

The security guard thanked me. He was so very thankful. I went out to the parking lot and had a cup of black coffee and a couple of American Spirits. When I came back an hour later, he was slumped on his little desk. I called to him, then I shook him, then I reached over and unlatched his holster. I took his service revolver and walked right into the clinic."

CHAPTER 30
My Ship

"My Ship," lyrics written by Ira Gershwin and music by Kurt Weill. It's a song of longing, and of waiting patiently for the beautiful things in life to finally come your way, but with it a reminder of how hollow those things are in the end, if you are alone. The instrumental version by Rashaan Roland Kirk and his quartet recorded in 1964 is itself a beautiful ship, as Kirk reminds us at the end that, "You've been aboard my ship... beautiful ship."

I HAD BEEN more or less stable over the next few days. During that time, Dr. Sanders would come to the ICU often to visit with me and to talk. It seemed as though we had crossed a bridge, some transition. There was no longer any hesitation between us. We were each very comfortable speaking openly to the other. She really wasn't interviewing me any longer. We were just talking.

There was no longer anyone stationed at my door. Even the detective had disappeared. Perhaps they had all given up on me finally, or maybe the writing was on the wall, and they knew that I wasn't worth the worry. They knew that I was dying.

"Let's keep going." urged Dr. Sanders. "Do you have the strength?" she asked.

"Strength can be deceiving," I said. "Bamboo is one of my favorite plants. I remember when I found some five-foot specimens at a garden center and dragged three potted plants to my pickup. I was parked next to this Mexican gardener's truck. He looked over at me and said, 'nice bamboo.' I think that maybe he and I could be the only two people on Earth who appreciate it. In the years that I've had it growing in my yard I have never had one compliment—none, since that one time when I dragged them like wild beasts through the parking lot. I can sit and stare at the bamboo for an hour, watching it whip back and forth in the wind. Most people warned me, 'Be careful with that,' 'I wouldn't plant that. It will take over, you know.' I never listened. Let it take over. It should. I love the lime green leaves on the yellow stalks, tough as nails. It's a survivor. That's why it's so beautiful. Can you build a home or a boat, a bridge or a fly rod or even a bicycle out of a weed? Yes, if it's bamboo. Others find it messy and unpleasant, but it will outmaneuver and outsmart and strangle anything in its way. It will build a thick forest that is impenetrable—a barrier to keep out what is not wanted. The stalks are thin and wispy at first, but quickly they harden. They are so tough, even when only as thick as a pencil."

"I'll take that as a yes." she said smiling.

"Did you recite the Hippocratic Oath when you graduated medical school?" I asked her.

"No, I didn't. Did you?"

"No. I always expected that it would be part of our graduation pomp, but it never happened. Actually, I think they stopped doing that in the 1970s. I guess we're not that old at least.

Primum non nocere. First, do no harm. It's really not even part of the actual oath. Did you know that?" I asked. "I always thought that it was the first line of the Hippocratic Oath."

"Me too," Dr. Sanders said.

"Did you know that in France medical students sign a copy of the Oath upon graduation. In many countries it is somehow incorporated into the ceremony. For us here, it's just implied. I think we should be made to learn it from day one. It really should be clear."

That enigmatic phrase can be traced back to Hippocrates though. "Of The Epidemics" is part of *The Hippocratic Corpus*—a collection of ancient Greek medical texts, written between 500-400 BCE. That's where it comes from. There's a lesser-known quote from the writing, which I recited aloud.

"The physician must be able to tell the antecedents, know the present, and foretell the future—must mediate these things, and have two special objects in view with regard to disease, namely, to do good or to do no harm."

It hurt to laugh, but I laughed a little, and so did she.

"How do you know that stuff?" she asked with a smile.

"We spent a lot of time in libraries, Gabriel and me."

"Those are quite high expectations that we've placed upon ourselves, that the universe has placed upon us," she said.

"I agree. The problem is that by its generality, it ends up being too vague. What constitutes good, and what harm? Left to the interpretation of us humans, like any creed or religion, you can guarantee that it will get completely messed up, and lose its true, original intention. But I'll tell you this, despite all of the imperfections and ambiguity, it meant something to me, and I have lived and breathed it. My entire career and even my life has been guided by that principle, even if it's not part of the damn oath."

"I suppose you might say that Gabriel represented the opposite, I mean that part of you that was resentful and dismissive of medicine and doctors."

"Yes, I think that's true, Dr. Sanders. There was always a conflict there, and it continued to escalate, until everything came crashing down."

CHAPTER 31
Bitches Brew

The natural course and conclusion, once it was all set into motion, the melding of jazz, avant-garde, and fusion. It's a constant stirring and whipping up, the results of which are a potion that is at the same time beauty and chaos. 1970, Miles Davis, *Bitches Brew*. It's like a twenty-seven-minute dream.

FROM DETECTIVE ROMAN'S interview notes with a liposuction nurse in the OR:

The doctor had a gun in the back of his waist and pulled it out when he saw the nurse come into the room with the proctor. He turned the music down and made me go and gather everyone and bring them back to the OR. I didn't want to. I just wanted to run, but I didn't. There was a new employee of ours that was young, and she was pregnant. I told her to run. As she flew out the glass door at the front of the lobby, I saw the security guard slumped over. I knew then that we were on our own.

When I returned with the other three, I could see that the doctor was agitated. He was pacing and yelling out loud to himself. He had tied up the patient on the table. He had everyone facing the wall. I was sure that he was going to kill everyone. We were crying. There was a gunshot. I screamed and fell to my knees thinking someone had been shot. Then there was silence. When I turned around, I saw that he had shot himself. There was blood all over his abdomen coming through his scrubs. His look then slowly changed to a strange smile. He raised the gun and walked toward the proctor. They looked at each other for a few terrifying moments. Then his arm went down to his side. He fell to his knees, and then over onto his side. He was almost unconscious. I kicked the gun out of his hand. He lay there murmuring something—something in Italian or Latin I think. I wasn't sure. The police arrived as he lost consciousness.

The paramedics put him on a stretcher and rushed him out of there. Another team took the patient, who seemed to be in shock. The rest of us just sat there, completely silent now.

Dr. Sanders was visibly uncomfortably as Gabriel recounted more of the events of that day.

"Look Ma, I'm a surgeon! I was finally a doctor. I was having a blast, one instrument in each hand. You'd think that an ambidextrous surgeon could make twice as much money, right?

The patient started jumping around when I tried to get started, and then *she* had to ruin it—that nurse. She came flying in there with the proctor, and I had to pull out the gun a lot sooner than I had planned. As much as I was digging that stupid song that was blaring through the speakers, I had to turn it down. I wanted everyone to hear me very clearly.

The OR was a small room, with only one door. I told the nurse, since she was so fucking good at recruiting people, she should go out and get everyone in the clinic and bring them into the room. I told her not to bother with the security guard, because he was napping, and that if she tried to play me and didn't come back, I'd start shooting people.

Now the naked patient was completely out of her mind. I had

to restrain her. I stood there and looked the proctor in the eyes. He was terrified, fidgety. I told him to be smart, and I slid the tray of scalpels out of his reach. I was tapping my foot to the pop music still playing on the speaker. When the music stopped, I realized that the nurse had gone out of range with her phone, so I fired a round into the ceiling. The proctor screamed, the patient screamed, we all screamed, although mine was the best. Then the nurse came back into the room with two other nurses and the receptionist. They were all crying.

Michael was in the room too, being useless, just standing there like an oaf. I told him why I had come back, why I had followed him here. I'd returned to punish him for everything that he'd done to me, for stealing my life, for pushing me aside, for putting me in that place. He thought that we could just pick up like the other times, forgive and forget, like nothing had happened? He was so pathetic now, alone, weak, it was almost going be less satisfying for me.

They were all backed up against the counter and around the corner against the wall. The patient was squirming and screaming. I leaned over her and told her that if she didn't shut the fuck up, I was going to kill her. She quieted down, whimpering a little. I was okay with that. I just needed to be able to hear myself think. I remember popping an oxy and chewing it while I figured out what I was going to do.

I had initially planned to pistol whip Michael in front of his staff so that I could humiliate him while they watched him beg for his life. Then a different idea came to me. *Why don't I kill each of them first and make him watch it all.* The surgeon, with his bullshit oath, and his lifetime of trying to help, or cure, or save people—that would be even worse than death for him. *Yes, that's what I'll do,* I thought.

So, I was about to do it. I had them all turn around and face the wall. Michael was begging me, pleading with me. He began bringing up all the good times we had spent together, the early stuff, and I started to listen to him. He was naming all the music we used to dig. It really made me smile. We had times that were pure and honest.

I froze for a moment with him, reminiscing, then he asked me to do him a favor, in honor of everything that we had been through together. He told me that I should kill him. He begged me to kill him. 'Pay me back for everything.' he yelled. 'Blow my fucking brains all over this place!'

I have to admit that this shook me. I started thinking that maybe he was right. I mean, why should these innocent people have to die? But you know what happened? The longer I stood there thinking about it, the more I remembered how I'd been treated, and how I'd been lied to, and discarded. I decided that I would put the two plans together. Yes, I was going to kill them all, but first, first I was going to shoot him, but guess what, I wasn't going to shoot him in the head like he wanted. I knew that if I was to put a bullet in his liver, he would die alright, but not for a while, not before he saw all the rest.

It felt good to have a plan, and it felt good to shoot him, to see that look in his eyes, first of surprise, then extreme pain, and finally acceptance. 'Don't go to the light yet my brother!' I yelled. 'Act two is coming up.'

I'm not sure if it was the excitement, or the oxy, or what, but I suddenly began feeling dizzy and weak. I remember thinking that I was so close. Then, BAM, that was it. Apparently, I had passed out. Do you believe it? I'm so pissed. I'm not sure if I finished them all off, or just Michael. I just don't remember."

"Can I tell the rest to you now? Fragments are coming back to me."

"Sure Michael." she said with some apprehension.

"When I came to, I realized that he must have done this to me. He was still there, in the clinic somewhere. I knew what he was capable of. I burst out of prep room and ran down the hall to OR 2. There was loud music playing and he was in there, all gowned up, about to start the procedure on that poor woman. He was singing. The nurse was terrified. Then she ran past me out the door.

He didn't acknowledge me but kept dancing around and singing. When the nurse came back into the room she had the proctor with her. They made a move toward him, and he pulled out this gun—he had a gun!

He made the nurse gather everyone else into the OR. He finally acknowledged me. He said that now was his time. He was in control now. He was going to make me pay for everything that I had done to him. He told me that he was going to kill them all. How could this be happening to me? My life's work had been slowly crumbling for some time now, little by little, but now, this was like an avalanche, as if my past and present and anything that ever could have been possible for me was all sheared off and falling into this darkness.

It sounds silly Dr. Sanders, but your life does start to flash by when you're dying. Time slows down. All of the memories, the long road, what was it all for? I had tried to appeal to Gabriel, to remember the good times we'd had, but he was unreachable. It seemed as though he was in a trance for a few moments, and then he burst out.

Then something strange happened. Although it was like a splash of cold water in my face, in some way I had known the truth for a long time. Reality was always shifting for me, but I suddenly found myself willing to accept one reality as fact—the reality that I was sick. My mind wasn't right, or it wasn't for this place. I had been wrestling with it for as long as I could remember. I was exhausted. I had to finally admit to myself that maybe Gabriel was me, and that I was Gabriel. What's worse is that I no longer had any control over him. I had always been able to keep him in check, but now he had taken over. I couldn't let this happen. Even if everything else in my life had gone sideways, I had always been faithful to my ideals. I had suffered to be true to those principles. If he was to kill anyone, it would really be me killing someone! I think that is what finally forced me to accept it. In the past I had always tried to keep him separate, put him away, run away. That was no longer an option.

I thought that if only I could convince him to kill me, it would, in fact, kill him, and I could save them. I begged him to do it, but he was cruel to me to the end.

I had always imagined that someday he would come up behind me and shoot me in the head. He wasn't kind enough to do that. Whoever he was now, was not who he had been, yet I could not be angry with him. He wouldn't go easily. He never could. No, instead he put the bullet in my liver knowing that it would keep me alive just long enough to see what he—what I-- had done.

"It must be hard to imagine a person with two people in his mind. I remember hearing that one should never be of two minds about anything, because neither will survive. I'm proof of that.

I can only be grateful that Gabriel miscalculated, and that I hemorrhaged so quickly that we lost consciousness before he could complete his plan. So, now, here I am alive—at least for now, in this hell, where reality is present only some of the time—the rest is left to my tired and sick mind to fill in the blanks. Those blanks are where the devil lives."

CHAPTER 32
Disambiguation

"Tezeta," 6:08. Mulatu Astatqe 1969. He is the Ethiopian born father of Ethio-jazz. A multi-instrumentalist, a composer, and an arranger, his *Tazeta* is a music genre of Ethiopian ballad. The word refers to nostalgia or longing—disambiguation. The twisting sax is searching for clarity, for explanation.

Dr. Sanders prepared her final report and submitted it to the head of the psychiatry department:

He had a way of seeing through people. It's like he could sit and listen to someone talk, and he could see right through the words. He didn't even need the words. He could read you. And I'm trying to piece it together; how could he be so good at that when his own mind was in such turmoil? How could he know when someone needed him—his skills, his help, his attention - when he never knew what was real and what wasn't? Maybe he learned to treat everything as though it was real, even if he knew that there was a chance that it wasn't. He was an empath. That's what got him from the very beginning.

Toward the end I spoke very frankly with him. I put it all out there. I was interested to know how his mind would process this new reality, now that he seemed to have surrendered, at least to the notion that he was mentally ill, and that he had no real gauge of what was real or what was delusion. I told him directly that Gabriel never really existed, that he had created this companion early in his childhood. From the day he lay there in that hospital recovery room bed, on one side was a horrifying and disfigured example of the pain and the cruelty—the reality of life here in this world. When he turned his head the other way, there was a calm and comforting friend. That's how early this started. The friend he created walked with him through every phase of his life. He was alone in life, but with Gabriel, he was never completely alone.

Unconsciously, he created a narrative—a dynamic that was a recipe for success, but they couldn't both succeed. That's where the conflict began. That's when Michael tried to distance himself from Gabriel—but their bond, their co-dependancy, was too strong by then.

It's funny, the stories he told me, so detailed, I didn't even know if any of it was real. It turns out that almost everything was factual. He merely inserted Gabriel into that reality. What's even more interesting is that in those stories, the most colorful and passionate details were the ones that he imagined, or that his illness created. He didn't only create Gabriel, but also Gabriel's family, his history, his neighborhood. Somehow, by attributing to Gabriel the very disease that he, himself had, Michael was able to separate that illness from himself, at least enough to enable himself to function at such a high level, until of course, he couldn't any longer.

I told him that I, indeed, was real, but the man who interviewed him in the restaurant, the detective that he spoke about, the guards at the door of his room, and even the nurses keeping watch in his room day and night—none of them, none, were actually real. He wouldn't argue any of it with me, but through his eyes, I could see his mind processing it all, accepting it.

There was a particularly touching conversation Michael and I had one day. He asked me if his family was real, his wife and children, and his dogs, or were they not. I smiled and assured him that they absolutely were. He wept.

"The people in the clinic, were they real?" he asked me next. I told him that yes in fact they were all real—the patients, the nurses, the receptionist, the security guard, even the proctor.

"And I saved them all? I saved them?"

"Yes Michael. They are all fine. When you decided to attempt taking your own life, you did in fact, save theirs."

In the end, he became very thoughtful, as if he was opening up his mind to me—giving it up to me—all of the swirling thoughts that had been in there all of these years, spilling out.

"These things that are wrong with me—or not right, at least—they weren't always bad, or at least not all bad. What I mean is that with everything that has come from this, there have been good things too, tender and sweet things."

"Yes, Michael. I think it is safe to say not all of your experiences were bad."

"Sometimes when I drive down the highway and I look around me, it is all so beautiful. The hills and the redwood trees, the rolling fog. I feel as though it's too beautiful to be real. I put my window down and reach my arm out to see if I can touch the mountain as I drive by, wanting to get the dirt and rock under my fingernails or catch a handful of fog. But I am not close enough to touch any of it. I wonder if any of it is real. I look over at the other drivers. Would it be strange to see them all with tears in their eyes like me, driving along in awe, like me—or is it strange that I am the only one? Am I the only one?"

Despite having struggled his entire life, he considered himself fortunate. He couldn't help but absorb and internalize those struggles that his patients endured every day. In comparison, he felt that his burden was light. He told me that he waited for a sign from God—a message that would guide him or tell him how to repay for all his good fortune in life. He felt that he had always been taken care of by some greater power. He thought that, as compensation, maybe he should have volunteered his skills in a war zone or a medical mission. Although he did charity surgery whenever he could, he never felt that he had done enough, and he waited for that sign, that direction, but it never came. That's how concrete his thinking was sometimes. I explained to him that maybe his mission, his way of paying back, was the millions of little things he had done all of these years. I told him that life is a war zone, and he had lived through plenty of it right where he was. He had been a good man and had cared for people.

Even at that point, after everything, there was something that still bothered him. He couldn't seem to get past how it had all ended for him—and Gabriel. He felt such sympathy for Gabriel, even to the end.

He always tried to build Gabriel up. He projected many of the positive aspects of his own personality onto him. I discussed this with him once.

"You were the one who read the Bukowski poems before bed every night, and you used that bookmark as a place where you could escape to, just so that you could fall asleep. You realize that right? Do you remember that?" I asked.

You know what he said? This was typical of those later days with him.

"You tell me doctor. If a flower struggles through the winter and pushes up through the icy clumps of frozen slush to catch the sunlight of spring, and to bloom in the heavy summer air, only to bend and die unseen in the mountain meadow's autumn, is that beautiful, or is it sad. Is it possible to be both? That's what Gabriel was. In the end, I don't know why that flower ever existed."

I understood and looked into his eyes. I told him that I thought that he was beautiful, that even if he had pushed up through the slush and nobody saw his summer, with all of his flaws and his delusions and his failures, even more so for all of them, that he was beautiful.

"Am I?" he asked, more as a comment than a question.

"Of course you are. These interviews, and what you have written have helped me to better know who you are."

I paged through some of his writings and handed one to him. He read it carefully, almost as if he didn't remember writing it. I could see the pain in his eyes as he read it. When he was done, he handed it back to me. He closed his eyes to hide the tears and lay back in his bed.

"I think we'd both like to meet the person who wrote that." he said. "Unfortunately, he's already someone else."

CHAPTER 33
On The Nile

"On The Nile" from the album *Jacknife*, Jackie McLean's alto saxophone leads the quintet, with Charles Tolliver on trumpet, Larry Willis on piano, Larry Ridley bass and Jack DeJohnette drums. Together they give a modal and exotic trip. Jackie's alto sounds like he's charming a cobra. Tolliver's trumpet is calling from afar as our barge drifts toward the distant shore. The trickle of the piano and the rhythm section is hypnotic, an oasis.

DAYS LATER, DR. SANDERS submitted one final addendum to her report:

"Rivers are easiest to cross at their source." That's an ancient saying from the Roman Stoics. Instead, Michael walked along that stream, and eventually the stream became a river, finally so broad and turbulent that there was no crossing it. Perhaps things would have been different if he could have had help early on, but his mind would not allow that. Society, and the field of medicine must bear some of the responsibility as well. For the mentally ill, there are more roadblocks to care than resources. The training of young doctors has evolved somewhat. The work hours are now limited by law. Still, our society and the profession itself place stresses and responsibilities not equaled in any other profession upon people like Michael, with very few resources to help them cope.

From a very young age, Michael found a way to overcome every obstacle, over and over, and over, but it finally broke him.

Michael and Gabriel died two days after our last visit. He knew that he was dying. I would like to say, and it would be poetic to say, that he was ready, or at peace. But he was neither. In his whole life he had never been at peace. He told me that he wanted his body to go back home, to Milwaukee, where the soil was soft, and there were clouds, and fireflies, and thunderstorms. He said that with any luck he could be buried in the rain, like Jesus was, and that the worms would come up to welcome him in.

The day before he died, he wrote me a note with an attached letter and asked the nurses if they would give it to me if he didn't get the chance to. The note said, "Thank you Dr. Sanders, for your time and interest. You once said that by understanding me you might better be able to help others. Perhaps there are lessons in the life I have lived that would benefit others. Thank you for all you have done."

Attached was the following:

Each day is not that much different from the last. Their accumulation however—the sum of those days changes things. As the waters of time round the stones in a stream, today is a little different than a day two months ago and more so a day twenty years past.

The mountain sits silent and seemingly unchanged. I live in its shadow, and most days I don't notice it. Sometimes, when the setting sun turns it on like a spotlight I do notice. I smile at first, then not. I sit in my car at the stoplight and my gaze follows the mountain road up its steep incline and switchbacks. In my mind I am on its peak, then flying down its descent. I haven't been there for a long time, a mountain of time.

At the edge of the road is a wild patch of weeds and climbing plants that have accumulated into an imposing mound of life. I see this mess some days. On other days it's invisible to me, like the mountain. I wonder if, behind those tangled brambles, within the impenetrable woven walls, there might be a beautiful garden—a garden that was planted with care and pain—the one who planted it, who toiled and suffered there, who smiled and rejoiced there as well, now long passed. I'd like to think that beautiful things and beautiful places always remain somewhere, somehow. Like the mountain or like a pyramid swallowed by the desert's shifting sands—sometimes we don't see them.

Perhaps they are not there at all. Perhaps they are in my windy mind only. When the light changes, the driver behind pushes on his horn, I move on. The mountain is gone, the garden, hidden once again.

I am not sure if this is the case, if others see these things, but I am at peace with that, with my virtual reality, with the mountain that appears and disappears, with the garden that defies suffocation.

www.ingramcontent.com/pod-product-compliance
Lightning Source LLC
LaVergne TN
LVHW041944070526
838199LV00051BA/2895